ROOMMATE R💋MPS

Love Thy Neighbor

TEAGAN HUNTER

Editing by Editing by C. Marie

Proofreading by Judy's Proofreading & Julia Griffis

Cover Design: Emily Wittig Designs

To bourbon.
Thanks for making 2020 tolerable.

Chapter 1

COOPER

"PENIS!"

My shoulders shake with laughter as I sit in front of my computer, plugging away at my latest project, a video game I've been working on for the last six months.

I don't want to get my hopes up or anything, but I believe it could be the game of the year when we're finished with it.

"Again?"

"Yes, again!" Her sigh carries through the apartment. "Just tell me what it is!"

"Why didn't you save it?"

"You know I'm not tech-savvy."

She's not wrong there.

Caroline Reed, my best friend since I was fifteen, is decidedly *not* the tech guru in our duo. I think if it weren't for me pushing her to always buy the latest versions of phones and computers, she'd still be rocking a flip phone and the world's thickest laptop.

She's the artsy one. I'm the buttons and clickies.

She's the hide-behind-a-book type, and I'd rather spend my Friday nights at the local sports bar.

We make no sense as friends, but here we are, living together in peace. Friends for...what has it been now? Ten, eleven years?

Either way, I can barely remember a time in my life before Caroline came barreling into it with her surprisingly smartass mouth.

"Just tell me the dang Wi-Fi password, Cooper! Or I'm going to call your moms and tell them you're looking up dirty things on the internet again."

"I'll tell them myself."

"I will beat you with my flip-flop!"

Okay, so maybe it's not as peaceful as I thought.

"Come on, Coop." She groans loudly, and I grin because I can imagine her face all scrunched up like it always gets when she's angry.

"You didn't ask for it correctly..."

"I NEED YOUR PENIS!"

Doesn't matter how many times she yells it—which is strangely often—it still makes me laugh like a maniac.

I could change the Wi-Fi network name from *Yell I Need Ur Penis 4 Password* to something else and make it a little more "family-friendly," more "mature," but where's the fun in that? Working from home all day long gets old quick, and I'll take my laughs where I can get them.

I push away from my desk and make my way from my bedroom/office into the living room, where I'm not surprised to find Caroline curled up under the massive gray blanket we've taken to calling the chinchilla blanket because we swear it's as soft as the pet she used to have. She acts like it's freezing in our apartment with just her face poking out of the mound of fabric.

"Give me your phone." I hold my hand out, towering over her huddled form. "And stop being such a baby. It's not even that cold in here."

"It's sixty!"

"You live in Colorado for fuck's sake and have for several years now. You've had plenty of time to acclimate to this weather. Quit acting like you can't take a bit of chill."

We originally grew up in Florida, where we were more accustomed to ball-busting heat than ball-shriveling cold, but we've lived here in Harristown in the mountains for about seven years now. We're used to this climate—or at least we should be.

"Or you could, I don't know, turn the heat up."

I quirk a brow. "I'm sorry...are you the one paying the electric bill?"

She grumbles under her breath. I can't fully make it out, but I'm almost certain the word *asshole* is in there somewhere.

"That's what I thought." I wiggle my fingers. "Phone."

"Just tell me."

"No, because I'm going to *save* it into your phone for a change so you're not bothering me for it tomorrow night, or yelling through our apartment about how much you need my dick when we're both painfully aware of how thin these walls are. You're already the talk of the morning mail run."

"Then change the Wi-Fi name."

"And ruin the fun for later? No way."

"Ugh. Fine."

She darts her hand out and settles the two-generation-old

brick into my hand, then quickly wraps the blanket back around her, chattering her teeth to try to make me feel bad.

Nice try.

I am way too cheap to fall for that shit.

I punch in her passcode, then enter the Wi-Fi password, making sure to hit *save*.

"There. Now you won't have to ask again for another month until I change it again."

"I don't understand why you change the password so often."

"Because I'm a paranoid computer nerd."

"You got the nerd part right."

I hold her phone up, shaking it. "Just for that, I'm keeping this."

"You are not. Give it back."

"Come get it from me."

She wrinkles her nose. "On second thought, keep it." She pulls her blanket tighter, if that's even possible. "It's too cold out there. Now move, you're blocking my view of *The Vampire Diaries*."

I glance behind me to the TV. "Again, Caroline?"

"Yes. They use my name in this show, *and* fake Caroline and I look alike. I'm required to watch it to support my long-lost twin."

I distinctly remember when the show first came out and Caroline called me over under the guise of studying when I knew she just wanted someone there to hold on to in case she got scared of the vampires.

In the end, she was more freaked out by the fact that the character who shares her name could easily be her older sister. She switched the TV off immediately and refused to ever watch it…until articles came out about all the shirtless scenes. Putting on a brave face, she overcame her fear of her small-screen doppelgänger.

The damn show has been on repeat since.

"Multiple times?"

"Yes."

"And it has nothing at all to do with the hot vampire douche-bros?"

"Douche-bros?" She narrows her eyes at me. "Don't act like you hate it. There have been *plenty* of nights you've watched it with me."

"Only because I'm a good best friend. And because you take the batteries out of the remote."

The brat *always* hides the batteries when she wants to watch something she knows I won't like.

Technically, I *could* change the channel from an app on my phone. But, shit, those fucked-up vampires and their shitstorm of drama suck you in.

Plus, you know, it's chock-full of hot chicks, which, if anyone asks, is exactly why I'm tuning in.

"You know, I—" Caroline's phone vibrates in my hand. I look down at the screen.

The fuck?

"Whoa now," I say, my interest piqued by what I see. "What's this we have here? A notification for Dud or Stud." I peek at her. "When did you get on that app?"

Her baby blue eyes—the ones that have gotten me in more trouble than I care to admit over the years—widen to about twice their usual size, and she shoots her hand back out from the comfort of her blanket cocoon. "None of your beeswax. Give me my phone back."

Her voice is up two octaves…and my curiosity rises along with it.

"Maybe I'll just…"

I swipe down, intrigued that my best friend is on a dating app and hasn't once mentioned it.

"Don't you dare, Cooper Bennett!"

Too late.

I've dared.

And I immediately fucking regret it.

MrSexMachine69: Are you sweet, Caroline? Because I can make you ba-ba-ba all night long.

And then there's a dick.

On my best friend's phone screen.

It's a small one, too. And fucking gross. Like "the guy should spend a little more time in the shower scrubbing it" gross.

My lips curl up in revulsion. "Is this the type of shit dudes are sending you on here?"

"What?" She shoves out from her warm haven and rises to her full five-seven height, then snatches her phone from my hand. "What'd he—*oh hell.* Not this guy again."

"Again?"

She groans. "Yes. He keeps making different profiles and I keep falling for it like an idiot, but I'd recognize that penis anywhere." She shoves the screen in my face. "See that mole on his stomach?"

I smack the phone away, glaring at her. "Can you not shove dick pics in my face?"

She shrugs, glancing back down. "You're lucky. At least he plucked the mole this time. Usually, you can see a few long black hairs sticking out of it."

"You are way too nonchalant about this."

"It's kind of par for the course." Another shrug. "Dating is weird nowadays."

"Just because we've moved to a more technology-based way of meeting people doesn't mean you should be subjected to unwanted pictures of rotten peckers."

"It does look rotten, doesn't it?" She shudders.

"Why do you keep falling for this crap?"

Her eyes narrow to slits as she looks up at me. "First, lose the judgment-filled tone."

"Lose the dick pic in my line of sight."

She shoves it in my face again, and this time I'm quick, plucking her phone from her hand and pocketing it.

"Cooper!"

"You can get it back when we're done with this conversation," I say, crossing my arms over my chest, staring down at her. "You're not answering my question. How the fuck do you keep falling for the same dude's shit?"

"What do you mean? It's all online."

"Yes, but—"

"It's not hard to create a new profile. It's not like the app gods keep good track of that stuff. There are *so* many people on here pretending to be celebrities. I once got matched with Tom Holland. It, unfortunately, was not him."

"Why do you say that like you talked to this catfishing dude for a while to determine it wasn't in fact Tom Holland?"

"Hey, I've read my fair share of romance novels—falling in love via a dating app or by accitext is a thing."

"Accitext?"

"You know, you text the wrong person on accident and then you fall in love. Accitext." She shrugs. "It happens."

"Yeah, in *fiction*."

"Fiction sounds really good right about now. It's a heck of a lot better than standing around listening to you judge me."

"I'm not judging you. I'm worried about you and the random dicks—actual random dicks—on this dating app you're on."

She rolls her eyes. "Please. Don't start your whole *big brother* bull hickey again. That's *so* high school."

I don't bother denying it, but I wouldn't call fending off numerous tools a *big brother* move, just a common sense one.

I saved Caroline from many shitty dates and handsy assholes. It's not that I completely kept her from dating—I'm not her parents, just a concerned friend—but I did do plenty of vetting and never let her forget it.

"You know, I'm surprised you aren't on the app with you being perpetually single and all. I'm sure you'd match with someone in no time considering…" She gestures toward me. "Well, you know."

I do know.

And that's not me being a cocky douche. It's the truth, and my physique is one I work damn hard for.

I can thank my middle school years for my love of hitting the gym, being bullied about being a tiny little shit when all my friends had already hit puberty and were shooting up like trees. I begged my uncle to allow me to use his workout bench in his garage for the whole summer between eighth and ninth grade. A month before high school started, I *finally* hit a growth spurt. It seemed like I sprouted four inches overnight…and then didn't stop until I hit six foot five and towered over everyone else.

I lift a brow. "Elaborate for me."

She huffs. "You know exactly what I mean. All buff and hot and whatnot."

That same brow inches higher.

Hot? That's a new one from her.

Over the years, she's called me cute or handsome, even dropped beautiful a few times, whatever the fuck that means for a dude. But *hot?*

That word has never left her lips regarding me.

I…think I like it.

I lift my lips into a smirk. "You think I'm *hot*, Caroline?"

Another glare. "You're something…like annoying, for one thing. You're totally ruining my vampire-fest right now, and you're a tool for taking my phone, which I'd like back now."

She holds her palm out again, and when I don't hand over her cell, she lunges for me.

I sidestep her easily.

She tosses her head back with a groan, her hands falling to her hips, where I can see her fingers digging into her flesh with frustration. I'm pushing all her buttons tonight, but I don't care. I want to know what she's doing on a dating app. The Caroline I've known for years has always lamented the lack of finding a real connection with someone. That's not something you usually get on some dating app, *especially* one like this.

"Come on, Coop."

"Don't you *come on* me. Stop trying to change the subject. What the hell are you doing on Dud or Stud? This app is like a breeding ground for douchebags."

"Um, trying to find a stud, obviously."

"Why?"

"Because I'm going to start dating."

"Why?"

"Because it's what people do."

"Why?"

She grits her bright white teeth. "Cooper…"

I raise my hands. "Just saying it's a little out of left field for you. You've been content living that…what's that saying you're always spouting off? 'Free and single, just don't make me mingle'?"

"Yeah, well, things change."

Sure. But not this. This hasn't ever changed.

She's been in about as many relationships as I have, which isn't saying much. She's always been indifferent to dating. Why is she going after it so hard now?

There's something she's not saying.

"Care…"

When she sees I'm not going to let her get away with a half-assed answer, she throws her hands in the air, frustrated.

"Because I'm lonely!"

There's a commotion from the apartment next door, and I have no doubt the old, nosy broad living there has her ear pressed up against our wall again.

That's the only problem with where we live. We're in the heart of the city, and there are a lot of older folks here whose rich kids have set them up in this hot locale because it's within walking distance of everything you could ever want. Which, in turn, means *a lot* of gossip floats around here because everyone is bored with their lives.

Due to the fact that Caroline yelled it louder than when she asked for the Wi-Fi password, I'm sure half the apartment building will have heard about how lonely she is by nine AM.

Fucking mailbox gossips.

"I'm lonely, okay? Are you happy?"

Not by a long shot.

Not when she stands there wringing her hands together, her nerves showing clear as day.

Not with her bottom lip tucked between her teeth.

And not when her blue eyes are turning sadder by the second.

An upset Caroline is my least favorite version of her.

Hell, I'd take an angry version of her over this.

This one makes me feel all protective...and something else I can't quite put my finger on, but I know I don't like it.

"Why are you lonely?" I point to myself, trying to lighten the mood and ignore whatever is eating at me. "You have me —is that not enough?"

"You're *you*, Cooper." She lifts her eyes skyward, a grin pulling at her lips. Then it's gone. "I'm lonely in different ways."

Oh.

It hits me all at once.

I know *exactly* what Caroline's after.

Dick.

"Sex," I provide helpfully, nodding.

Her cheeks redden, and I smash my lips together, trying not to laugh at her reaction.

Caroline's always been shy, but she's especially timid when it comes to discussing anything sexual. I remember the first time we watched a movie with a sex scene in it together, though I use "watched" loosely because she kept her eyes closed the entire time.

She still watches them that way.

I've teased her about it—mercilessly, I might add—over

the years, just to get a rise out of her. At the moment, though, I can see she's feeling vulnerable, and it's not the time.

She lifts her shoulders.

I cross my arms over my chest. "What does that mean? That shoulder shrug of yours."

"It's typically the universal sign for *I don't know.*"

"How do you not know if you're referring to sex?"

Her eyes narrow once again. "It's my not-so-subtle way of telling you to mind your own business because I am *not* talking to you about my sex life."

She's my best friend and I know her better than anyone. If she really didn't want to talk about this, she'd be running for her room, not standing here looking at me with those eyes that say *Help me.*

And I'm just *that* kind to help her out.

"Are you just trying to get your rocks off, or are you wanting to find a boyfriend or whatever they're called these days?" Another blush. "Because if it's the latter, dating apps are *not* where you want to go searching. Ninety-five percent of those guys are just looking to hump and dump."

She scrunches her nose. "That's an awful saying."

I shrug. "But a true one."

"Is that what you call what you do? Humping and dumping?"

I wince. When it comes out of her sweet mouth, it sounds extra awful.

But, yeah, I'm guilty of it. In fact, it's how I operate. One-night stands, going back for seconds here and there. Aside from the one girlfriend I had in high school, and unless you count the two long-term—if carrying on for less than three months is long term—bed buddies I've had, the no-strings thing has always been my thing.

I'm not one of those guys who's trying to do everything in his power to not be tied down. I just haven't found someone who's worth it, and I'm not into false hope.

Until I'm ready to give someone my all, what's the point of playing house?

"We're not talking about me."

"Clearly, Mr. Avoid the Subject."

"We're talking about you," I continue, ignoring her all-too-accurate accusation. "Dating or fucking?"

"I am *not* answering that."

"Ah, so rocks off it is."

"Stop." The color on her cheeks deepens.

"I can help, you know."

Her brows shoot up. "With what?"

"Your problem."

"My…problem?"

"The sex thing."

She runs her tongue over her bottom lip. "Are you saying you want to…have sex? With…me?"

She freezes, and I don't dare even blink.

All the air in the room is sucked out at her question.

Time stands completely still.

Then, it cracks.

Or we do.

We double over in laughter.

I already made the mistake of trying to take things to the next level with Caroline when I was a horny teen who was basically into anyone with a great rack—something my best friend definitely has, not that I've officially noticed or anything.

Either way, my experiment failed. *Epically*.

It solidified that friends are all we're meant to be. Any time I get an inkling of an idea that we're meant to be together in some crazy stars-aligned way, I think of that failed kiss.

She wipes under her eyes, brushing away the tears that always form when she laughs too hard.

"Oh wow. I haven't laughed that hard in way too long. I needed that." She barks out another laugh. "Can you even imagine? Taking a romp in the sheets with you? Pass. *Hard pass*."

Ouch.

I try not to take her words too harshly but, *fuck*, a man has his pride, and she just landed a direct hit to mine.

She sounds disgusted by the idea of us together, and while I can manage rejection just fine—not that it happens often—I wasn't expecting *that* reaction.

Sure, I get it…to an extent. It's one thing to strip bare with someone you hardly know, but it's a whole different story to do it in front of someone who sometimes knows you better than you know yourself. It makes it ten times more personal.

I'm sure that's what she's referring to, but it's damn hard to not take offense at her words.

I'm not lusting after her or anything, but I'm also not completely immune to…well, *her*.

Caroline Reed is hot, and if she were anyone other than my best friend, I'd have tried to woo her into my bed long ago.

I'd be a bald-faced liar if I said I never thought of her in ways that aren't…appropriate.

I don't think the idea of us together sounds *that* bad.

I let my mind wander for a split second, conjuring up those images I keep locked tightly away and have only indulged in a few times over the years.

Us. Naked. In bed together.

Caroline's blonde hair wrapped around my fist with her on her knees.

My face between her thighs.

My—

Wait—no! Stop it, you dumbfuck. This is Caroline you're thinking about. You're best friends. You do not cross that line, no matter what. Tuck that shit away and don't you dare let on that your dick is starting to react.

I give myself a mental shake, pushing it aside, praying my brain won't decide to replay that later when I'm attempting to fall asleep.

"It's nice to know your mind is firmly in the gutter tonight, but I meant more like helping you find some suitors. Come out with me tomorrow."

I already know what her response is going to be—a solid no—but it's a million times better than her idea of using this stupid app.

Speaking of...

I navigate to her apps folder and promptly uninstall the damn thing before that sicko sends another nasty picture of his dick.

"With you? On a Friday? In...public?"

Okay, that's the second time tonight she's sounded repulsed by me. Now I'm *really* starting to take it personally.

I peel my eyes from her phone, narrowing them at her. "Don't say that like you think I'm disgusting."

"*You're* not. Your friends are."

Mostly true. They kind of are dicks. And gross. Especially when they get more than two beers in them, which is basically every Friday because those nerds get out of the house less than Caroline does, and that's saying something.

Why the fuck do I hang out with them again?

Oh. Right.

Team building, as my boss likes to call it.

"What if I promise it's just the two of us?"

I can totally ditch them...I hope.

She twists her lips. "I don't know, Coop. I haven't been out in a long time."

"All the more reason to go." I shake her phone in my hand. "You want to get laid? Let's find you someone."

Besides, I could use a few hours away from my computer, as well as a pair of legs wrapped around my waist. It's been far too long since I've gotten laid myself.

"That's what I was trying to do before you ruined it."

"Let's do it the old-fashioned way—by *talking* to someone."

With a shaking hand, she tucks an errant strand of hair behind her ear.

It's her tell. She's nervous because she's not good at the talking thing...and because she's considering my offer.

"Come on, Care. What do you have to lose?" I pull my lips up on one side. "Besides your virginity?"

"I am *not* a virgin!"

"Are you sure your hymen hasn't grown back?"

"Okay, that is *not* how it works and you know it. But, if that's your way of implying it's been way too long since I've gotten laid, you're right."

"Good. Then we agree. You're coming with me tomorrow." She opens her mouth to argue, but I point a finger, silencing her. "You're going." I toss her phone back to her. "And that's final."

"Don't boss me around like you used to do in high school."

"You love it when I boss you around."

She grumbles something, but I don't catch it. I'm already back down the hall, almost to my bedroom. If I'm going to spend the night out with Caroline trying to teach her how to get some, I need to get ahead on work now because I will need *a lot* of drinks to get through it, which means I'll do fuck-all on Saturday.

"If I go—and that's a *big* if—you're buying drinks! And I am *not* doing karaoke!"

Chapter 2

CAROLINE

"BOSSY JERK." I shake my head. "Nope. Bossy *ass*. Yeah, Cooper Bennett is an *ass*."

I slip my gray chinchilla-soft blanket around my shoulders, cocooning myself back into its warmth, and crawl onto the couch to resume my state of *I've had a long day and all I want to do is be a bum.*

"Bossy *cheap* ass too," I add, my teeth beginning to chatter because my once cozy blanket is now cold. I was out of my haven for too long. I'm freezing again.

I'd say I can't believe Cooper won't turn the heat up, but the man is so tightfisted when it comes to the bills. If I even dare leave the water on for more than two seconds when brushing my teeth, he's there to turn it right back off and scold me for *running up the bills* like I don't pay my fair share too.

I don't understand where he gets it either. It's not like he grew up fighting to get food on the table or struggles his way through life now with his cushy video game developer job. There's no solid reason for him being so stringent with his money other than wanting to make me miserable.

Who am I kidding? He probably gets off on bossing me around just like he has since high school.

We attended the same schools since kindergarten and had several classes together, but we weren't what you'd describe as friends. Hell, I wouldn't have even called us acquaintances. Cooper had his friends and his admirers from playing every sport he could sign up for.

Me? Well, I had my books. And I was happy in my own little bubble of quiet.

We didn't truly interact until my parents went through the world's most amicable divorce and I moved before the start of our freshman year. Not wanting to uproot me from a school district I'd been in my whole life, my dad—who I opted to live with full-time—moved us right across the street from my now best friend.

And Cooper being Cooper took it upon himself to "take me under his wing," which apparently meant forcing me to put my books down and talk to actual humans.

Much to my initial dismay, the guy never left my side. But eventually, I grew used to him.

He can be overbearing, sure, but on the other hand, he's helped me overcome my perpetual shyness in many ways, so I guess I can't bemoan him too much.

"Thank you...*ass*," I mutter.

"I know you're not in there mumbling about how much you hate me," he singsongs from his bedroom.

"You're right. I'm just gushing over how much I love you."

Not.

"That's what I thought!"

With a roll of my eyes, I point the remote toward the TV

and press play, turning my beloved vampires back on, trying to drown out my best friend's clacking away on his keyboard.

"And don't roll your eyes at me!"

"Are you spying on me or something?"

"No. I just know you that well."

I do it again just to spite him.

The episode continues, but by the third time I've rewound a scene, I realize my mind is about a million miles away.

Instead of focusing on the fictional love story playing out before me, all I can think about is my sad excuse for a love life.

And that's just what it is—*sad*.

I can't remember the last time I went out on a date. Or even had a guy ask me out. Hell, I can't remember the last time a guy was even *interested* in me for anything other than sex.

Cooper's right. The dating apps I'm willing to sign up on —AKA the free ones—are full of dudes just trying to *hump and dump*, as he so elegantly put it. It's not really my style. I've always been a relationship kind of gal, but if relationships aren't working, maybe I should give something else a shot? Coop has no problem doing the one-night-stand thing. Perhaps I need to take a page out of his book, get him to teach me how to do a one-night stand.

Is that even how you say it? Do a one-night stand?

See? *That's* how out of the loop I am on dating. I don't even know the proper terminology.

It's been one craptastic experience after the other. I blame my underwhelming dating life on Tommy Wilson, my first boyfriend from the ninth grade who kissed me so aggressively he chipped my front tooth with his braces. I won't even mention all the saliva involved.

Apart from my second kiss, which came from Cooper and was completely accidental (but still counts), my dating experience has been lackluster at best.

I've had a few boyfriends here and there, but nobody who has come close to being *the one*.

I'm sure being painfully shy doesn't help my abilities to hook a guy one bit, but it's just who I am.

My mother used to tell her friends it was just a phase, and every time she'd say it, I'd swallow those words down, praying they'd sprout trees inside of me and help me bloom into someone who didn't want to puke at the thought of social interaction.

They never grew.

Here I am, a twenty-five-year-old who'd much rather spend my Friday nights curled up on the couch watching perpetually teenage vampires fall in love with silly humans than go out and interact with actual real people.

People disappoint. Vampires are forever.

I should make a shirt for that.

Just the thought of designing has my fingers itching to pick up my sketchbook, and without any care for how much I'll regret it, I slip out of my warm cocoon. I grab my pencils and old, torn, beat-up pad from the bar, then sprint back to my blanket before I lose my limbs to frostbite.

Back under the covers with my book in my lap, I flip open my most treasured possession, grab a pencil, and let my mind take over as my hand begins to fly over the page.

Designing has been my outlet for stress since I picked up the habit of reading. I always had a tough time imagining how the characters looked in certain scenes. As most preteen girls understand, my mind would always get stuck on what the character was wearing. Is she wearing a cute summer dress or sweatpants when talking to her crush? What exactly does a pair of *fuck me* heels look like? I *needed* to know to build the world inside my mind.

After years of burning through notebooks and ideas, Cooper's moms taught me how to sew, and I soon started making my own stuff, starting with my prom dress in my junior year of high school. I was dead set on art school for college.

My dreams were stomped on before they even got off the ground.

My dad called it a pipe dream. He refused to pay for something so "impractical" and wouldn't allow me to apply to any design schools.

So, I put my sewing machine away and earned a bachelor's degree in education.

It took all of one year after I graduated to know I was *not* cut out to be a teacher. I was miserable, and there was no way I was going to be able to make a career out of it if I wanted to keep my sanity.

Much to my father's dismay, I called it quits. Two weeks later, I stumbled into Making Waves, the unique, fashion-driven boutique I've worked at for the last few years.

Though my boss, River, would love it and weekly tries to get me to agree, I can't seem to muster the courage to sell my designs at Making Waves.

I'm terrified I'll fail and be left at square one.

If my own father couldn't believe in me, why should anyone else? His lack of faith in my ability to pursue my dream of becoming a designer killed my spark so much that I put my sketchpads away throughout college, focusing on something practical and attainable.

Not until Cooper encouraged me to quit my teaching job and I was hired at the boutique did I start designing again.

While I still create my own clothes now, I'm a lot more private about it.

Which is exactly where I'm at with dating too.

Why put myself out there when I can stay in and enjoy the comfort of television and delivery service? What's the point?

God, I sound so bitter and pitiful.

Like a broken-hearted fool, although I've never opened myself up enough to have my heart broken.

Maybe Cooper's right. Maybe I do need this.

I wasn't lying when I said I was lonely. It's just not entirely in the way he's thinking of.

My loneliness isn't entirely bedroom based. Honestly, there's a good chance I'd be just fine with my vibrator getting me off the rest of my life.

It's alone in other ways. The subtle ones.

The handholding. The giggling over something only you two find funny. Someone knowing how I take my coffee and getting it for me before I even ask. The looks across the room that say *Let's get out of here.*

The small stuff nobody really thinks about.

I didn't even realize it was something I was missing and wanting until I had to see it firsthand all the time.

A few months ago, River and her incredibly hot boyfriend, Dean, finally put us all out of our misery and gave in to the whole *will they/won't they* thing they had going on after Dean almost burned his apartment down and River took pity on him, letting him stay with her. Their forced proximity brought their true feelings front and center, and after finally admitting where their affections lay, they've been together since.

They still bicker like an old couple who's been married for fifty years, but they're sickeningly sweet together...and I'm jealous of it. What they have is something I never thought existed outside of romance books or movies.

My parents didn't exactly have a picture-perfect marriage, though it wasn't the worst thing in the world. There was no yelling or fighting. It was something much quieter.

Cold.

They were that couple who dated for a while and discovered they weren't compatible about the same time they found out they were pregnant, then stayed together because it was "the right thing."

Practical, they said.

I wasn't at all upset when they sat me down to tell me they were getting divorced. It was a blessing in disguise. Not just because I no longer had to watch them suffer in an unhappy marriage, but because it led me to Cooper.

The Bennett family took me in. Showed me love. Showed me how a family is supposed to function.

I'd never give him the satisfaction of knowing it, but sometimes I think Cooper was the best thing that ever happened to me.

Which is why we both know I'm going to agree to go out with him tomorrow. He's never led me astray before...as long as you don't count the time he turned me into a thief by telling me the olives in the olive bar at Publix were free. I stole them for over three months before someone caught us. Cooper laughed himself silly while I was humiliated, getting called into the manager's office and given a stern talking-to.

Like I said, *ass*.

My hands come to a natural pause, and I glance at the full sketch I've done for the first time since I started drawing. I realize I've made the perfect dress for tomorrow night.

A rush of adrenaline courses through me and I start to feel excited about the outing.

Okay, fine. I'm thrilled about my creation, not the peopleing part.

With the euphoria making my fingers itch with the need to make something, I rise from my spot on the couch and dash toward my room, fully absorbed in my new design.

I'm not paying any attention to where I'm going and fly around the corner, only to run smack into the wall.

"*Oof.*"

Why is the wall talking?

Why is the wall *wet*?

Why does the wall smell like sage and warm summer nights like Cooper's bodywash which I definitely do not ever use or smell in the shower?

"Don't move," he warns, his voice low and quiet in my ear.

The hairs on the back of my neck stand on end.

It's the same voice he uses when there's something behind me that I don't want to see.

Fear consumes me, and everything happens at once.

Scared, I jerk backward, and for some reason, Cooper follows, falling into me. His heavy hands land on my shoulder and stay for half a second before he's shoving me away.

Something brushes against my leg and I panic, sending

my sketchpad into the air and landing I don't even know where.

His towel, which has apparently attached itself to the broken spiral that's barely holding the pages together, is tangled up with my book that's sprawled out on the floor down the hall.

Cooper's standing opposite me.

Naked.

Completely and utterly naked.

Is that his...

Oh my.

It is.

"Fuck."

His voice is raw. Hoarse. Totally not him.

His hands fly to cover his junk, and the tic in his jaw is unmissable. A storm brews in his usually pale green eyes, and I'm not sure if it's due to anger, humor, or embarrassment.

I don't watch them long enough to find out.

Completely unable to be stopped, my eyes travel of their own accord.

Down his straight nose, over his chiseled jaw that's always lined with at least two days' worth of stubble, and over his throat that's bobbing with every thick swallow.

There's a smattering of hair on his chest, and it surprises me. More so, it shocks me how much I like it.

I've always found myself more attracted to smooth chests when scrolling shirtless guys on Instagram, but there's something about seeing the hair on Cooper's chest that screams *mature*.

My fingers itch to touch it as much as they do the tight, well-defined abs I know he spends a lot of time on.

A knot takes shape in my throat, and a throbbing that I haven't felt in far too long begins between my legs.

Cooper looks good. *Really* good.

No! No. Stop it!

Slamming my eyes closed, I swallow the lump and ignore the pressure building in the parts of me that haven't seen action from anything other than my vibrator for a year or more.

Neglect.

That's all it is.

I'm gawking at Cooper of all people because I haven't had sex in far too long.

It's not him. It's just my desperation.

Or maybe it's just that I'm shocked to see him like this.

In all the years we've been friends, this is *definitely* the most naked I've ever seen him. I can count on one hand the number of times I've seen him without his shirt on, and that's usually just a glimpse when he's left his bedroom door open or his shirt gets stuck to his hoodie when he takes it off or when swimming, but it doesn't count when all the dudes at the pool are shirtless.

It's an unspoken agreement between us. We keep things like nudity to a minimum. Not because we're afraid we'll jump the other's bones at the first sight of skin, but because we acknowledge the stereotype that comes with our friendship.

You can't be just friends *with the opposite sex.*

It's total baloney, of course. We're proof of that.

And that's exactly how I know the ache that's still between my thighs is nothing but pure human instinct and has nothing at all to do with Cooper himself.

There is absolutely *no* chance it's anything to do with Cooper.

I'm sure of it.

I'm hot. My face is on fire. And I want nothing more than for the earth to open and swallow me whole.

I can feel Coop staring at me.

"Well, this is unfortunate," he finally says.

I nod.

He chuckles.

"Open your eyes, Caroline."

I shake my head.

"Come on. Let's not make this more awkward than it already is."

With a deep inhale, I peel my eyes open.

"You know, if you wanted to see me naked, all you had to do was ask."

My eyes widen to twice their normal size, and he laughs.

I swear I can feel the rumble down to my toes.

"Cooper," I whisper, completely mortified. I haven't been this embarrassed since he forced me to be his date to a homecoming game and I tripped in front of the entire school when he escorted me across the football field.

I try to will away my blush, but I know it's pointless, especially with Cooper smirking down like he is, his full lips pulled up on one side and a sparkle in his pale green eyes.

I'm tall, but Cooper towers over me like I'm the smallest thing ever.

"I'm sorry." He sounds anything but. "Let's just go to our rooms and pretend this didn't happen."

I nod. "I'd like that very much."

"You go left. I go right."

I move.

He moves.

We collide, tripping over one another, limbs tangling in our awkward dance.

And I definitely touch his dick.

We freeze.

My back is against the wall, and he's caging me in. He drops his head to the spot next to mine, and I try not to drop my gaze to see what's hanging between us.

"Are you *trying* to kill me?"

He swallowed glass—or at least that's what his voice sounds like.

We're quiet, and I'm not sure either of us has taken a breath.

My blood is pumping so hard I can't even hear the TV playing in the other room anymore.

Time is standing completely still, and I wonder if I fell asleep on the couch and this is just a crazy dream I don't ever want to repeat.

"Okay." He exhales sharply, and another "*Fuck*" drops softly from his lips. He's so close I can feel his stubble scratching against my cheek. "I'm going to go to my room and go to bed. To make up for fondling me, you're going to say yes to going out tomorrow night and buy me drinks to help me cope with my trauma. Got it?"

I nod, not trusting myself to speak.

I mean, I *did* just accidentally grope him. He deserves drinks.

"Good. I'm going to walk away now. *Do not move*," he instructs. "And listen this time."

Another nod.

He pushes off the wall, and I slam my eyes closed again.

I don't dare open them until I hear his bedroom door bang shut.

I run to the bathroom and push the door closed, locking it behind me for good measure.

I lean against the sink, dropping my head between my shoulders, taking what feels like my first real breath in hours.

Don't think about it. Don't think about it.

I turn the faucet on to the coldest setting and splash freezing water on my face until all thoughts of Cooper and his —*nope! Not thinking about it.*

I do it again. And again.

I don't stop until my face is numb and my mind is blank.

Only then do I dare to open the bathroom door and slink out into the hallway with my eyes closed, too terrified to open them and see the spot where our friendship was rocked to its core.

I don't open them again until I'm in my bedroom, my back pressed against the closed wooden door.

The boundaries we've carefully laid out were just blown to bits. Every line we've ever drawn was crossed.

It'd have been one thing to see him naked. It was bound to happen at some point.

But friends don't look at each other the way I looked at him.

The throb between my legs hasn't subsided, and I'm so keyed up I'm not even sure pulling out my sewing machine and working on my new design is going to relax me.

Images of a naked Cooper assault me.

His long, bare body.

Perfectly toned. Perfectly lickable.

I gulp and crash my hands through my hair, lifting the mass of blonde locks and fanning at myself.

You're just all worked up because of talking about your sad love life. It has nothing to do with Cooper himself. Just desperate, remember?

Yeah, yeah. That's all it is.

It's fine. Everything is fine. You're just going to pretend it never happened and you'll laugh about it later. Stop thinking about his dick. Stop thinking about him. You're going to go out tomorrow and get laid and you'll never think about this again and it'll be fine.

An all-too-familiar *click* echoes through the quiet apartment.

Cooper's door creaks as he peels it open. He pads out of his room with determined steps, so loud, like he's stomping, though I know he isn't.

He pauses, and I can see the shadows of him dancing across my floor. He's mere inches away from the door, and for a second, I pray he just walks away.

"Fuck," he mutters yet again.

I hear him suck in a deep breath, and a soft thump hits the door. I know it's his head making contact.

Without making a sound, I spin, pressing my ear against the door. I relish the feel of the cool wood against my otherwise clammy skin as I wait for him to say something.

Do I even *want* him to say something?

What is there to say at this point?

Hey, look, I know you just saw me naked and touched my dick, but it's your turn to set the coffee pot for the morning.

He clears his throat, and I hold my breath.

"I didn't think you'd take it so literally."

I pinch my brows together and pull back, staring at the door, confused as hell.

Take what so literally?

"I'll change it tomorrow."

Curiosity beating out my mortification, I pull the door open, and Cooper stumbles backward.

The moment my eyes meet his, I dart them away, looking at any place but him. The awkwardness hangs between us like a dense fog, and those freakin' images I don't think I'll ever be able to get out of my head come back again.

I slam my eyes closed again.

Breathe, Caroline. It'll be fine. Just breathe.

"First thing in the morning," he says, cutting through my thoughts.

My brows draw together tighter, and despite the blush creeping into my cheeks, I peek up at him.

"What are you going on about? Change what tomorrow?"

His eyes dance with mischief. "The Wi-Fi network name. I didn't think you'd take it so literally."

Son of a...

Yell I Need Ur Penis 4 Password

And just like that, I feel lighter as a slow grin stretches my lips.

Things are going to be just fine.

Chapter 3

COOPER

CAROLINE SAW ME NAKED.

It was the last thought that ran through my head before I finally passed out around two AM, and it was my first thought when the early-morning sun poked through my blinds half an hour ago as I peeled myself out of bed.

It's the same thought that followed me into the coldest shower I've ever taken.

The thought is still running through my mind as I rinse out the coffee carafe from yesterday, getting ready to start the first pot of the day. First pot, because I'm damn sure I'll be having another one today.

I chased sleep like I've never chased it before just to quiet my head, and the bitch eluded me all night long. I think I got around three hours if you add up all the times I wasn't wide awake with my mind running wild.

My best friend who has always safely lived on one side of the line we've mutually agreed to saw me in nothing but my birthday suit.

Fine. Whatever. So it finally happened? Big whoop.

It was bound to happen given the number of years we've known each other. We could have gotten over it after a few days of not making eye contact. She'd say something silly and I'd make fun of her and we'd be fine.

Except Caroline didn't run. She didn't hide. Didn't even cover her eyes.

No.

She stared.

And I mean *gawked.*

Ogling me like I was her favorite ice cream flavor and she was being handed the last scoop.

I can't remember the last time a woman looked at me like that. It took every ounce of willpower I had to keep my dick down as much as I did. I thought of every awful thing I could conjure, and I *still* rose to half-mast just from her stare alone.

Then, she brushed against me.

And I died.

In that short millisecond in the hall, I felt my heart stop beating.

I couldn't think. Couldn't move. Breathing was out of the question.

I just couldn't decide if it was because everything I had with my best friend had just changed…or because it was being challenged.

You're being dramatic, you moron. Just don't make a big deal out of it. You made her laugh with your joke last night. She's over it. You're over it. You're both moving on.

Right. Moving on. That's what we need to do.

Her bedroom door clicks open, and I freeze.

Just like I know she freezes when she sees my bedroom door is open.

34

She knows I'm awake. I know she does because I can hear her sharp inhale from here.

Time to face the music.

I imagine her pushing her shoulders back, charging forward with all the false confidence she can gather, and padding down the hall.

She appears around the corner, her blonde hair a curly mess, her favorite pair of tattered jammies hanging off her like they always do.

She looks normal. The same. Like nothing at all has changed between us.

See? It's not a big deal.

Then our eyes meet, and her cheeks turn bright red.

Yeah, it's *definitely* a big deal.

I clear my throat.

"Coffee?" I ask, trying to push forward and act like everything is fine.

Maybe if I pretend enough, it'll be true.

"Please."

I nod, reaching for the coffee beans from the cabinet above the coffee station we've created. I pour the desired amount into the grinder and turn it on.

From my peripheral, I see Caroline move through the apartment and into the kitchen. I try to ignore her, focusing on getting the coffee from the grinder and into the filter and pressing start on the pot.

The legs of the stool scrape noisily across the floor, the sound breaking through our silence. She hauls herself up onto the seat and rests her elbows on the counter, looking anywhere but at me.

I lean against the counter, as far away from her as

possible.

I can't help stealing glances at her as she picks the polish off her nails. Then moves on to pulling at the strings of her worn pajamas, still avoiding looking at me.

She looks nervous, and Caroline hasn't looked nervous around me since we first met the summer before high school.

I recognized her from school almost instantly. She was the girl people whispered about when there was no other good gossip to go around.

She was so quiet back then. It's not that she isn't still quiet now, especially around people who don't know her, but back then her shyness was ten times worse. She lived inside the pages of her books, and it was near impossible to get her to talk to anyone.

When she moved in across the street, something in me screamed to talk to her.

I "accidentally" threw at least ten balls into her yard the first two weeks she lived there. Not once did she look up from her book. It didn't matter how close anything came. She was oblivious to them.

So one day I stomped over there and stole her book.

She talked to me then all right. Yanked her book back and told me to stick it where the sun doesn't shine.

Being the absolute dumbass I am, I did it again the next day. And the next.

I was there every day until she finally gave in to my advances, taking pity upon a bored neighbor kid and talking to me.

We've been inseparable since.

Through all the awkwardness of high school, first kisses, and first dates, the loss of innocence. Through first car wrecks and heartbreaks. Hell, we even survived college together for fuck's sake.

But this? It's a whole different kind of difficult to navigate, and it's the exact reason we had those lines. The exact reason we stayed on our respective sides.

Thoughts like this begin to creep in, and you can't control them. You're suddenly thinking of ridiculous things like how soft your best friend's hair looks while you're trying to make your morning coffee.

The timer sounds, signaling the brew is finished, and I push off the counter, heading toward the caffeine I'm in desperate need of.

Yeah, that's it—I just need a good dose of caffeine.

These ludicrous notions have nothing to do with last night and the thoughts that lingered in my head until the wee hours of the morning.

"Big cup," Caroline requests quietly.

I peek over at her, surprised.

Unlike me, Caroline isn't a caffeine-aholic. One small cup can get her through an entire day while I down at least a pot, sometimes two depending on the extent of the latest project.

"You want the big cup?"

She nods. "I need it today."

Another blush steals up her cheeks.

"Thank fuck." I blow out a relieved breath, so fucking glad I wasn't the only one up all night.

"You too?" she asks, her voice full of hope as she comes to life for the first time this morning.

Nodding, I reach into the cabinet, pulling down the bigger cup she requested, and begin filling it with coffee.

"I didn't fall asleep until like two AM."

"Me either!" she says, nearly coming off her stool in surprise and probably relief. She clears her throat, tucking a stray hair behind her ear, settling back down into her seat. "My brain wouldn't settle down. It was all I could think about."

Pausing mid-pour, I raise a brow at her. "It was?"

Her eyes widen as her words reach her own ears, and then she rolls them. "Not like *that*. I meant all I could think was *Crap, did we screw this up?* Repeatedly. Stuck in my brain like a time loop." She rubs her temples, then drags her palms down her face. "Did we screw this up, Coop?"

I can barely make her words out since she's hiding behind her hands.

I finish pouring our coffees and replace the pot. I grab both mugs, keeping one for myself and sliding the other across the counter to her.

She doesn't reach for it.

With a sigh, I move our cups to the side and lean across the bar until I'm just inches away.

"Care, look at me."

"No."

"Caroline Beatrice Reed, look at me."

She laughs lightly. "You know that's not my middle name. I don't know why you change it every time you use my full name."

"Because Agnes doesn't fit you and we both know it."

"And Beatrice does?"

"No, but it makes it more fun."

"True."

I reach out and wrap my fingers around her tiny wrists,

pulling her hands away without a fight. I grin when I see her eyes are screwed tightly shut.

"You better look at me or I'll tell your dad you snuck out of the house to make out with Bobby John in the tenth grade."

She groans, peeling her eyes open. "Bobby John—what an awful name."

"You kissed him knowing his name."

"Don't remind me." She curls her lip, then tucks it between her teeth, looking at me with those baby blue eyes that always get me to do anything she wants.

This time they aren't filled with a plea to watch some obnoxious teen drama, but instead, they're begging me to reassure her our friendship is intact.

"We didn't screw it up."

There's an inkling of relief creeping into the corners of her eyes, but she's still scared.

"Promise," I tell her. "In fact, I think it's good we now both know how much you want my cock."

That blush I've come to love over the years creeps back in, but for the first time in our friendship, I'm wondering if it's because I'm teasing her, or because I said cock.

There go those thoughts again...

Her eyes drop to my hands on her wrists, and suddenly it feels different to be touching her like this. More intimate somehow, even though I've touched her plenty before.

I slip my hands from her body and push myself away, grabbing my own cup of coffee, needing something to fiddle with to distract myself.

"You're an awful friend, Cooper Bennett."

"No I'm not. I'm the best friend—*your* best friend. And that's not going to change just because you saw me naked."

A slow grin pulls at her lips. "And touched your penis."

Fuck. I'd almost forgotten about it for a few seconds.

I smile back over my mug and play along. "Yes, and grabbed my massive, crazy impressive schlong."

"Was it massive? Huh. I was actually thinking it was kind of small."

I narrow my eyes at her. "Bite your tongue, woman." *I'll show you small.* "No wonder you're single, going around telling men their dicks are small. That's no way to get laid. But you know what a good way to get laid is? Going out with me tonight."

She groans. "Ugh. Don't remind me of that. I only agreed because I accidentally fondled you."

"Accidents don't just happen accidentally, Caroline."

She twists her full lips up in annoyance, reaching for her mug. "I'm so glad I decided on the big mug if I'm going to have to deal with you and your twisted logic tonight."

"Yeah, well, you better hydrate too. Don't forget you're buying, and, baby, your best friend is a lush."

"Oh, you don't have to remind me." She blows on the hot liquid in her cup. "I've taken care of your drunk ass enough times to know you can't handle your alcohol."

"Please. I can drink you under the table."

"Because I hardly ever drink. My tolerance isn't as good as yours."

"Thought you said I couldn't handle my booze."

"Not as in you vomit all over the place—you can't handle it in the sense of how much you drink. *That's* your problem." She takes a sip from her mug, sighing contentedly as the coffee hits her system. "Speaking of tonight, where are we going?"

"Probably Lorde's, that place that plays their music too loud but has really good drink specials. It's where we pretty much always go on these nights out. The boss loves it."

Another groan. "I thought you said we were going to be alone."

"I've been thinking about that actually. We can't go out alone."

Her mouth drops open. "Because I saw you naked?"

"What?" I shake my head. "No. We're over that already." *Lie.* "I meant we can't go out alone because then it's going to look like we're on a date. And if it looks like we're on a date..."

"Then I can't get laid." She nods and takes another drink. "That makes sense. But—"

"No!" I point at her. "No. When you say *but* like that, it means you're going to follow it with—"

"Counteroffer." She says it like I never spoke. "How about instead of going out with your douchebag co-nerds, we invite River and Dean?"

As much as I would prefer that... "Then we'll look like we're on a double date."

"Ugh. True." She huffs. "Fine. We'll just go out with your friends."

"You say that like I *want* to go out with them or something."

"You say that like you're not friends with them."

"I *have* to be friends with them. Boss's orders."

"Your boss is so weird, forcing you all to go out and be social."

"It's called being normal. You should try it sometime."

She taps her chin, pretending to think it over. "Hmm...no,

41

thanks." She takes another drink, smirking at me over the rim of her mug. "What are you making me for breakfast?"

I bark out a laugh. "Making you for breakfast? *I'm* the one who gave you a free show last night. *You* owe *me* breakfast."

She glowers. "Are you going to hold this whole thing over my head for the rest of our lives?"

"Yes. In fact, I'm marking it on the calendar as a special occasion. We'll commemorate this day for years to come."

Back in high school after Caroline got her first boyfriend, she—like every other teenage girl with a boy on her arm—became *obsessed* with arbitrary dates and anniversaries. For a moment there, she reminded me of Leslie Knope from *Parks and Recreation*, having a special date and anniversary for every little thing.

The first time Bobby John took me to get ice cream.

The first time Bobby John winked at me.

The first time Bobby John picked his nose and didn't eat the boogers.

Okay, fine. The last one *might* be made up.

But it doesn't detract from how real her weird fascination was.

Being the good best friend I am, I relentlessly made fun of her and made a calendar just for us. Whenever I started to remind her of our anniversary of the time she accidentally farted when she laughed too hard watching *Shrek*, she quickly got over her obsession.

It was too late because it was way too much fun to stop.

So, we didn't.

We're a little pickier about what we add to our calendar, but we still continuously update it and celebrate each day accordingly.

This one is definitely going on there.

She sighs defeatedly. "I hate how quickly you answered that."

Taking another big gulp from her coffee, she hops off the stool, lifting an eyebrow my way. Her hand is on her hip and she's staring at me with those *Don't test me* eyes, reminding me of all the times she called me an ass for stealing her books when we were kids.

"Fine. I'll buy you breakfast and drinks tonight, but starting at midnight exactly, it's in the past. Got it?"

I tap my heels together and stand ramrod straight, saluting her like a soldier in formation. "Yes, ma'am."

She shakes her head. "I'll get dressed. Breakfast in twenty?"

I nod, and she skips from the room, looking much happier than she did when she first entered.

I exhale the breath I feel like I've been holding since she walked in and scrub a hand through my hair.

We'll be fine. Everything will be fine.

I pluck my phone from my pocket and navigate to the calendar.

Everything will be fine. I'll make sure of it.

Chapter 4

CAROLINE

I'LL NEVER TELL my boss this to her face because I'm about seventy-five percent certain she'd fire me on the spot, but I much prefer cake to pie.

That said, even though The Gravy Train, an old train depot turned restaurant, is famous for its pie and twenty-four-seven breakfast-only menu, it's still one of my favorite spots in the city solely for their waffles.

When Cooper said I owed him breakfast, my stomach growled at the thought of stopping by The Gravy Train.

Standing here waiting in line to place our order is making it roar even louder.

It's a welcome distraction from all the thoughts of last night trying to barge their way into my brain.

I will not think about last night. I will not think about last night.

I have that sentence on permanent repeat, scrolling through my mind front and center like a movie marquee.

"Was that your stomach?"

"I'm *starving*. I ate dinner super early last night and then was too scared to creep out of my room for a snack."

His smirk makes me regret bringing it up.

But it's not a lie. I was too nervous to leave my room last night. I lay awake for hours trying to forget what happened. It was no use. The whole incident was burned into my brain.

And when I wasn't awake thinking about it, I was dreaming about it until I forced myself awake.

The cycle repeated.

"You act like such an old lady sometimes, eating dinner at four. *Wheel of Fortune* isn't even on then." He shakes his head, thankfully not commenting on our hallway mishap. "Let me guess, you had soup for dinner, didn't you?"

"It was cold in our apartment!"

"Old lady."

"Soup is *not* an old-person food."

An actual old man in front of us turns around with a grin.

"Did someone say soup? I have a bowl of some great homemade vegetable at home." He pats his belly. "I already can't wait for dinner."

I give him a smile, and Cooper—poorly—hides his laugh with a cough.

As soon as the old man turns back around, I smack my idiotic best friend.

It sends him into a coughing fit, drawing the eyes of many patrons, several of whom happen to live in our apartment building.

It's in the heart of the city, and we're aware every day just how lucky we were to score it. Almost all the occupants are older and come to The Gravy Train for breakfast every day.

Which also unfortunately means whatever happens around the apartments becomes the hot gossip at the diner.

It's a small price to pay for being within walking distance of just about everything you could ever want and having the best building manager on the face of the planet.

Cooper bends down, his lips so close I swear I can feel them brush along the shell of my ear.

"Told you," he whispers, and I do everything I can to hide the shiver that races down my back.

After last night, having Cooper so close to me feels different and makes me think of things I shouldn't be thinking of. Like how good he smells. Or how warm he feels.

I will not think about last night. I will not think about last night.

"Caroline?"

I turn toward the quiet voice, and Cooper turns with me.

Jason, a guy who frequents my favorite bookstore, is standing near the to-go window.

"Jason. Hey. How are you?"

"Good. Better now." He smiles shyly.

I met Jason a couple months back browsing the fantasy section. We literally bumped into each other. We laughed about it and he helped me pick out a book.

I saw him again the next week.

Now we run into each other at least a couple times a month.

He's a sweet guy. Quiet. A little shy. Traditionally handsome and very much the *take home to meet the parents* kind of person.

There have been a few times I've thought he was going to ask me out, but then he didn't.

I was a little disappointed at first, but over time I've learned to not get my hopes up.

Besides, the more I run into him, I'm not so sure he's my type. As ironic as it is, he might be a little too shy for me.

Cooper clears his throat.

"Oh, duh." I smack my forehead. "Where are my manners? Jason, this is my best friend, Cooper. Coop, this is Jason. He's another regular at *Books & Things & More*."

Jason gives Cooper a shy smile, while Cooper gives him a once-over.

I've seen Cooper act all big brotherly over the years when it comes to other guys. Always stepping in and sizing them up, making sure they're up to his standards of who he thinks is worthy of my time.

But this?

There's something else in his eyes I can't quite put my finger on.

"Next," the cashier calls.

"Well, that's us," I say, hitching my thumb toward the counter. "It was good seeing you, Jason. I'm sure I'll run into you next week too."

"Always a pleasure, Caroline."

He tips his head, grabs his order, and pauses once more to smile at me before leaving.

"That dude wants to fuck you."

"Cooper Ryan Bennett!" I admonish, smacking my hand over his mouth as he stares after Jason. "What is wrong with you?"

He peels my hand away, lifting his strong shoulders. "What? It's true. Dude totally wants to bone you but is too pussy to man up and ask you out."

"You don't know that."

"Brain." He points to his head, then to his nether regions. "Penis. Trust me, I know what I'm talking about. But you can't go there."

"What? Why not?"

Not that I'm sure I want to, but it's not his place to tell me otherwise.

"You said he frequents your favorite bookstore, right?" I nod. "Well, what if he ends up being a total loser and you hate the sex? Then you've just had a bad dickin' and you lost your favorite nerd hangout."

Shit. He's probably right.

But I'm sure Jason can't be that bad...

"Stop thinking about it. Just trust me on this." He places his hand on the small of my back and guides me toward the counter. "Good morning, Darlene."

"Hey, kids," she greets, flashing us a smile. "Want your usual today?"

"Yes. A vanilla waffle with chocolate chips, chocolate sauce, and extra whipped cream for her, and four scrambled eggs, fruit, and wheat toast for me," Cooper tells her like he has so many times over the years. He points to me. "Oh, and a chocolate chip cookie since she'll be paying this time."

Darlene lifts her brows, a grin pulling at her lips. "And here I thought you were a gentleman."

"I am. She just groped me last night and owes me."

"Cooper!" I shout, smacking him again.

He clutches his stomach, from laughter and from the pain I've inflicted.

I turn to Darlene. "Please ignore him. He fell last night, hit his head really hard, and is now suffering from assholeism."

Darlene nods, grinning. "My ex-husband had that too. I completely understand. Coffee's on the house this morning." She narrows her eyes at Cooper. "*Her* coffee. We just so happen to have run out."

"Of course you did." Cooper grins. "That's all right, Darlene. I see whose side you're on."

She shrugs. "Us girls have to stick together. Especially when we have people with assholeism in our lives."

I pay for our breakfast because I do still owe Cooper even though he's a jerk, and we make our way to the same spot we always sit in when we come here.

I spot River and Dean already sitting there, two slices of pie in front of them as she glares at his bent head. He's invested in his breakfast, and River's invested in burning a hole through his skull.

"Hey, guys," I say, approaching the community table. "What are you doing here, Dean? Shouldn't you be at school?"

"Parent/teacher meetings today. I didn't schedule my first one until later so I could have breakfast with this one." He sounds annoyed as he hitches his thumb River's way.

She rolls her hazel eyes at him.

Cooper and I exchange a glance as we take a seat at the table.

What's up with them? Cooper's eyes say.

No clue, mine answer.

I'd say I'm surprised they're arguing this early, but it's them. They're always arguing over something…then making up like they're sex-crazed teens.

I clear my throat. "Did we interrupt something?"

"Just Dean being Dean," River answers, brushing her long

dark red hair behind her shoulder and throwing daggers at her boyfriend.

The man in question tosses his fork down onto his plate, the utensil clattering loudly. He runs his hands through his messy midnight hair, though you'd never be able to tell because that's how he always wears it. During the week when he's teaching English to fifth graders, Dean is way more buttoned up than he is now, minus the always messy hair.

"What exactly is that supposed to mean, River?" he asks, his eyes narrowed on her in exasperation.

"It means you're just being you." She shrugs, her off-the-shoulder top slipping further down. "You know, a total jackass."

"How?! I gave you the cherry pie this time!"

She leans across the table. "You can't seriously think that makes up for what happened last night."

"Jesus, River. Is that what this is about?" He pinches the bridge of his nose between his fingers. "It happened. Get over it already."

"What happened?" Cooper asks.

"Dean *accidentally* watched the season finale of the show we've been bingeing without me."

"I didn't mean to!" he argues. "It auto-played. It's a good show. I couldn't look away."

"For *two whole episodes?*" River sasses back, pushing her nearly empty plate of pie away from her and crossing her arms over her chest, pouting at her boyfriend. "While I slept *right* next to you?"

"I said I was sorry *and* I got you pie this morning."

"I don't know, River—I think pie makes up for it. Plus, accidents happen."

My mouth drops open. "Accidents happen, Coop? What happened to accidents don't just happen accidentally?"

"That's different."

"How?!"

"Because you groped me."

Dean and River both turn to me, their eyes wide with surprise.

I close my eyes, wishing again for the second time in less than twenty-four hours that a hole would open up and swallow me down to the pits of hell, because I'd much rather be there than sitting here with everyone staring at me.

I can *feel* Cooper laughing across from me, and like the mature adult I am, I kick at him under the table.

When I don't make contact, I peel my eyes open and look underneath. The bastard is smart and must have known it was coming because he's *just* out of reach.

He bends, meeting my angry stare.

"Sorry," his mouth says, but his eyes say something else entirely.

I shake my head at him, pushing myself back upright.

"Um, Caroline," River says calmly, amusement dancing in her eyes, "care to explain what your dimwitted best friend is going on about?"

"Hey!" Cooper says defensively. "Why am I in trouble?"

"Because I'm mad at Dean and men suck."

"Sorry, man," Dean says to Cooper.

"Stay out of this," River barks at him before turning back to me. "What's he going on about?"

"It's nothing," I say quietly.

"That doesn't sound like nothing," Dean pushes.

Another glare from River.

"I guess Caroline finally gave in to her sexual urges regarding me and just couldn't stay away any longer." Cooper tips himself back in his chair, smirking like he's the funniest man in the world. "She caught me coming out of the shower, got a good look at my hot man chest, and couldn't help herself."

I curl my lip. "Nobody says hot man chest."

"But am I wrong?" he counters, still grinning.

"Yes!"

"What really happened?" River asks.

I explain to her the events from last night, and she's a good enough friend to not laugh until I finish telling the story.

Then she can't *stop* laughing.

"It's not that funny," I grumble.

She gets her giggles under control, fanning her face. "It really is though."

"She has a point," Dean says, chuckling. "I mean, what are the odds of all that happening?"

"You two don't even know what a klutz I am."

"Especially when she gets all flustered. It's awful. One time in college we were in the dining hall and some guy she'd been crushing on winked at her. She flipped out, sprung from the table, ran smack into some kid carrying a tray of spaghetti. She was apologizing like a maniac but in so much of a hurry to get out of there when she realized everyone was staring at her that she slid on the noodles and busted her ass in front of the whole cafeteria."

Oh hell. I remember that. It was *awful*. Not just because I fell, but because I pulled a muscle in my back and my butt was bruised from the impact. I walked to all my classes with a limp for days.

I get so flustered and my heart gets to racing so hard my brain just short-circuits and chaos ensues. Last night won't be the last time it happens, I'm sure.

"What'd you guys do after it happened?"

"Had wild, *wild* sex, of course."

"Cooper!" I scold for what feels like the millionth time this morning. "Stop it! I feel like you're just trying to embarrass me now."

"Well, duh." He shrugs, grinning. "That's what best friends do."

I actually love that he's been teasing me about last night.

I think it helps pull the seriousness away from it. Makes me feel like it truly wasn't such a catastrophic event, like we're going to be just fine and things will be back to normal in no time.

"We just went to bed," I tell them. "It's not a big deal."

I don't miss the way River and Dean look at each other, their eyes saying something I can't quite decipher but want to so badly.

Luckily, I'm saved from any other line of questioning by Darlene. She sets my cup of coffee down on the table and places a glass of water in front of Cooper.

"On the house," she says sarcastically.

He tosses her a wink, taking a big gulp from his glass. "Thanks, beautiful."

She shakes her head at him, waltzing away and muttering about him being an ass but a cute one.

When she's far enough away, Cooper reaches over and snags my coffee from me, swapping it for his water, knowing intuitively I won't want another cup today.

"So," I say, pressing on and away from the subject of last night, "what are you two doing tonight?"

"Well, I'll probably be groveling for at least the next three days, so we'll likely be having—what was it, Coop?" Dean snaps his fingers. "Ah, yes. Wild, *wild* sex."

River ignores him but also doesn't bother denying it. "Why? What's up?" Her eyes spark. "Are you going out with one of those guys from Dud or Stud?"

"Ew." Dean wrinkles his nose. "You're on that app? That place is a breeding ground for creeps."

River pins him with a stare. "How would you know?"

"Nolan," he says, referring to his best friend. "That horndog is on every dating app there is *except* that one. Even he won't touch it."

"First of all," Cooper starts, folding his hands together and leaning across the table with accusatory eyes directed at me, "I want to know why River knew you were on Dud or Stud before I did."

I lift a shoulder. "Because she helped me set my profile up."

"You didn't think *I* could help you set up your profile? I know you way better than she does."

"Hey!"

"Besides, have you seen her dating history? It's awful."

"Double hey!" River says a little more sternly this time.

"No offense, Dean."

He shakes his head. "None taken, man. I know she got lucky with me."

"I hate you both." River grabs for a packet of sugar and tosses one at her boyfriend.

He catches it with ease, then rips it open and swallows its contents.

"Ah, refreshing," he says enthusiastically, running the back of his hand across his lips.

"I can't believe I kiss you."

"I can." He winks.

He sends his girlfriend a grin, and the corners of her lips twitch before she groans, turning her attention away from him.

Cooper points to Dean, the disgust clear in his eyes. Other than getting an occasional chocolate chip cookie, he's not a big sweets fan, so I'm sure watching Dean swallow a packet of pure sugar makes his stomach turn. "You trusted River with dating advice when the guy she's dating just did *that*? Man am I glad I deleted that app from your phone and we're going to go out the good old-fashioned way tonight to get you laid."

"You're going out with Cooper?"

"Okay, why do I feel like you're saying that in a bad way?" he says to River.

"Because I am. You're a manwhore. It was my idea to not tell you about the dating app."

"I am not."

Darlene appears again, two plates in her hands. "You kind of are, honey. I've seen you in here many times with that *I got laid last night but I'll be damned if I know her name* glaze in your eyes." She sets a plate in front of him, then me. "And this poor girl is always sitting there looking like you dragged her out of bed in the wee hours of the morning to fix your problems."

She pats his shoulder, then promises to check on us in a few and walks away.

55

"See? Even Darlene knows you're awful with dating." I cut into my waffle, scooting it around the plate to make sure I pick up the fallen chocolate chips.

I try to keep my sweet tooth in control, but these waffles get me every dang time.

I take a bite, loving the way the vanilla flavor explodes on my tongue.

"Because I don't date."

"Because you're a manwhore," River supplies.

"No, because there's no point in dating if you're not ready to make something happen with the person. I'm not saying I need to date to marry, because I'm not a fool and life happens, but what's the point if I have no intentions of something lasting more than a couple months?" He shrugs, filling his fork up with another bite. "If I don't see years' worth of potential in a person, I don't pursue dating."

River twists her lips. "Hmm. I guess I actually kind of get that. You don't want to get either of your hopes up."

Cooper nods, shoveling a bite of his breakfast into his mouth, chewing, swallowing. "Exactly. I mean, come on, how often when you meet someone do you know straight away it's just not going to work?"

"Often," Dean says, seeing his point.

"Yep. But just because I don't want to date someone doesn't mean I can't spend an hour or two between the sheets with them." Cooper grins wolfishly. "You know, just to be sure."

"So you two are going out on the prowl tonight? You're going to, what, teach our shy girl here how to be like you?" River asks.

"Yes," I answer. "And you two are more than welcome to

come. Actually, I strongly encourage it. I really don't want to hang out with Cooper's douchey co-workers all night long."

River frowns. "Wish I could say yes, but we have plans tonight. Dean's sister, Holland, is coming into town and we're meeting her for dinner. Then I have some store stuff to catch up on and Dean has papers to grade."

"Ugh." Dean groans, tossing his head back. "Please don't remind me. If I have to read one more book report on Harry Potter, I'm going to scream."

Dean's an English teacher, and I have to give him major props for it. It takes a lot of love and patience to be able to do it. I should know—I failed at it spectacularly.

"Dude, I'm not a big reader and even *I* love Harry Potter."

Dean shakes his head at Cooper. "It's not that. Harry Potter is great, a fucking classic. But how is it seriously *every single student's* favorite book? There's no way. Plus, it would help if they didn't write their report on the movie version instead of the book. It's painfully obvious they didn't read it and just watched the film."

"The book is always better," I interject, wiping at my mouth with my napkin.

"That's why you're my favorite, Caroline." Dean holds out his fist, and I bump it.

"Okay, now that you two are done bonding over your mutual book-nerd tendencies, I have to get to work." River pushes her chair back from the table and stands. "I wanted to go over the books before we open."

"Which means I need to get to work too."

I take one last bite of my waffle and shove my plate toward the center of the table. I chug the rest of my water, then rise from my chair.

"Don't you dare let her work late and bail on our thing tonight," Cooper says, pointing to River.

"Please. If anyone is going to be dragged out of that place kicking and screaming, it'll be me. I'm married to my work."

"Which means I never have to propose." Dean pumps the air with his fist.

"You're so annoying." River shakes her head, rounding the table toward him. "But I love you anyway."

She places a kiss on his lips.

I force myself to hold back my sigh.

These are the small moments I want, the ones that are second nature to couples.

The breakfast dates in the morning. Dinner dates at night. The goodbye kisses. The way they look at each other with love when it's clear they're annoyed with one another.

"Hey, where's my goodbye kiss?" Cooper teases her.

"Right here on my ass waiting for you."

Dean laughs, then smacks said ass.

"Come on, Caroline. Let's go before I strangle your best friend this morning."

She wraps her arm around my shoulder, leading me away from the table, and I wave to the guys. Cooper holds his fingers up.

Eight.

That's when he wants to head to the bar.

I nod and he grins, and I could just be imagining things, but I swear I see it waver.

As soon as we're on the sidewalk in front of the diner, she spins toward me.

"Okay, spill."

"Spill what?"

"Last night. What really happened after the whole 'you seeing your best friend naked' thing?"

I will not think about last night. I will not think about last night.

I groan. "Nothing. It was nothing. I promise. Just something that happened."

She studies me hard, arms crossed over her chest, lips twisted up as she considers my words.

Please, please, please do not see that I totally had inappropriate thoughts about my best friend last night. Please.

"Okay," she finally says. "I'll believe that if you want me to. But just know, I'm here to talk if there's anything that's suddenly on your mind."

There is absolutely nothing suddenly on my mind.

Not Cooper. Not his incredible body. Definitely not his co—

"Nope. Nothing," I tell her, cutting off my own thoughts before I travel down a road I'm trying hard to avoid.

She nods. "All right. Well, why don't we talk about you going out tonight, then? Are you nervous? I know it's been a while since you've done the whole dating thing."

"Yes and no. I'm sure Cooper will take care of me just fine."

"Hmm," she says, lips tucked together.

"What?"

"Huh?"

"You said *Hmm* all cryptically—what's that supposed to mean?"

"Did I?" She waves her hand. "It was nothing. Come on. Let's cross here."

She starts rambling on about Dean and his betrayal last night, and my mind drifts to other things.

Again.

I will not think about last night. I will not think about last night.

How many times is it going to take until it's true?

Chapter 5

COOPER

"FOR FUCK'S SAKE, Caroline. Come on already. I've got two idiots from the team texting me asking where I am. How are you not ready yet? You've been in there for over an hour already."

"Five more minutes, I swear!" she calls from her bedroom.

With a groan, I toss myself back onto the couch and close my eyes, settling into the comfort of the well-worn cushions. Five more minutes my ass. She said that ten minutes ago.

After breakfast—and Dean asking at least ten different questions about last night—I came back home to a shitstorm of emails and work.

I've been cleaning up coding messes all day and barely got my shit done in time for us to be going out.

Now Caroline's taking ten months to get ready for a night out where she may or may not get laid.

I'm ready to drink. Relax a little. Maybe even get my own rocks off. I could use a way to blow off some steam.

I won't lie, I was a little grateful to come home to such a

mess with work. It meant I didn't have time to think about what happened with Caroline. It was a distraction.

Sitting here waiting on her?

It's too much free time.

She needs to get a move on so I don't do something dumb like start thinking about things I shouldn't be.

"Ready."

I peel my eyes open.

And *fuck me*.

Being best friends with someone for so long, you see all sorts of looks on them. The awkward seventies-retro phase. The choker and combat boots chapter. Even the *Is that a dress or my mom's shower curtain?* stage.

The girl—no, the *woman* standing before me isn't going through any of those anymore.

Caroline looks good.

Not the girl-next-door kind of good she always is.

More like *I'm going to ride you all night long* kind of good.

A wine-red sweater dress is hugging her body like it was made especially for her.

And it probably was.

I heard her sewing machine running last night when I couldn't sleep. I imagine she was in there working on this dress.

And holy hell did she knock it out of the park.

Caroline is a good designer, but sometimes she's timid, letting her insecurities hold her back.

There wasn't an insecurity to be found when she made this.

The neckline is deep, plunging where the dress wraps around her waist. Her tits are on display, but not enough to make her look desperate for attention. The dress is cinched at her waist with a simple sash, and it's the perfect accessory, accentuating the curves she spends too much time hiding beneath loungewear.

Her long legs look even longer with the tall black boots she's paired the dress with. Her lips are painted a dusty pink and her blonde hair is styled in loose curls that hang down her back, just begging to be pulled.

Sexy.

That's exactly how she looks.

Dangerously so, too.

Caroline isn't playing around.

She's out to fuck...and I kind of want to be the first in line.

The *only* one in line.

No. No lines. This is Caroline. The same one who was there when you got grounded because your moms found out you stole a porno mag from the gas station.

"What? What's wrong? Is it the dress?" Her timid voice interrupts my thoughts.

Her fingers are on the hem—because it's that short—nervously playing with it.

I clear my throat. "It's nothing."

"Are you sure? You're looking at me funny."

Because I think I want to fuck you and I shouldn't.

"Sorry. It's not you." *Liar.* "I'm just ready to get a drink in me."

She nods, tucking her hair behind her ear.

I sigh and push up to my feet, hoping and praying she

can't see the excitement happening behind the zipper of my jeans. "You look fine."

Fine? You fucking moron.

"Uh, thanks...I think." She wrinkles her nose, then gives her head a shake. "No. Not thanks. *Fine*? I put a lot of work into this dress and you think it's *fine*?"

"I didn't mean that. I—"

"Should I change?"

Yes, because it makes me think shit I have no business thinking.

"Do you think it's too much? Do I look desperate?"

"No. You'll definitely turn heads."

Too fucking many.

She grins. "Good. I mean, I *am* trying to get laid, so I thought dressing up a little was warranted."

Right. That's why we're going out. For her to get laid.

Because Caroline and I are *just friends*.

That's it.

End of.

No more inappropriate thoughts.

I need to get laid too. That'll get it all out of my system.

No more bad thoughts about my best friend.

I give her the biggest, most charming smile I can conjure and saunter toward her.

"Let's go get you laid."

"THIS WAS A REALLY BAD IDEA."

The worry in her voice is clear as her lips brush along my ear.

We've just stepped into Lorde's, my boss's favorite haunt, and she's already itching to go home.

I can't say I blame her. The place is more packed than usual, and that's saying something because the lounge/karaoke bar is a popular place to be on any given Friday night.

"It's way too crowded in here. If I even try to go to the bathroom, I'm going to get lost."

I reach down and grab her hand, linking our fingers together like I've done so many times over the years.

I don't miss how different her hand feels in mine tonight. How her thumb moves back and forth over that meaty part between my thumb and forefinger.

Have her hands always been so small and soft?

"I've got you," I tell her. "Just don't let go."

She nods, but the worry is still flashing in her eyes as I lead her through the sea of drunks and find our usual table at the back.

About a year and a half ago, my boss realized he could save a hell of a lot of money on rent and sent us all packing out of the office and into our houses. It didn't take long before someone complained about feeling too lonely not being surrounded by co-workers all day. Thus, our Friday nights out.

We meet at least twice a month, usually every other Friday, have a few drinks, and shoot the shit. It's our way of staying connected without having to smell each other's farts all day long. Not everyone comes each time, but there are usually at least ten of us.

"Hey! Bennett made it!" Paul, another developer on my team, holds his beer in the air. "Good to see you, man."

It's the same thing he says every time I see him.

"Hey, man," I say, shaking his hand with my free one. "How you been?"

"Not bad. Not bad at all." His eyes drift to Caroline, then down to our joined hands. "But not as good as you apparently." He leans into me. "About time, dude," he says, loud enough for me but not Caroline to hear.

Paul's been my closest friend since I started at the company. He's a good guy and has been over to the apartment a few times, and he's one of the few who's met my best friend.

He's been on my ass about the two of us from the moment he met her, always swearing something was going on that I wasn't telling him about.

There wasn't.

There *isn't*.

"It's not like that." I laugh, pulling back and dropping Caroline's hand like it's on fire.

I motion for her to step into the fold. She takes a tentative step forward, the attention of the whole office all on her. "Guys—and Joan—for anyone who hasn't met her yet, this is Caroline, my best friend."

"Hey," one says.

"Hello there," from another.

"Damn."

Someone even whistles. I think it's Joan.

Several of them mutter things I can't make out, which is probably for the best, but not a single person isn't looking at her with piqued interest.

And I don't like it one fucking bit.

My chest feels tight, like something I haven't felt before, and I'm already regretting bringing her out.

"She's off-limits."

It comes out harsher than I intend, but the wide eyes and nods from my co-workers tell me my point has hit home.

"Uh, hi," Caroline says softly, giving the group a wave.

I can feel the nerves radiating off of her, and I'm sure she's dying to dart away.

I lean down to whisper to her and regret it instantly.

She smells like apples, and I know she's wearing that perfume I bought her two Christmases ago. She only ever wears it for special occasions, and I guess tonight called for it.

I wonder if she tastes like apples too.

The thought slams into me.

I grit my teeth, trying to ignore the asinine idea of doing something I know I'll regret...like taking a taste.

"If at any time you're feeling overwhelmed, we can go. Just say the word and we'll leave. We'll grab ice cream and watch *The Vampire Diaries* and chalk it up to a bad experiment. Okay?"

I pull back, finding her eyes.

She's grinning at me, probably liking that idea very much.

"Maybe you're not such a bad friend after all."

If only she knew the thoughts I'm having about her...

"Told you." I wink. "Now, what do you want to drink?"

She tilts her head at me. "Are you really asking?"

"No, I guess not. You always get the same thing." She nods. "Okay, I'll be right back," I tell her.

"What!" she squeaks. "You're leaving me?"

"Yes, but I'll be right back. We can't be together all night, remember? You're trying to attract dudes. I'm hot, Caroline—I'll ruin all your chances at getting anyone to talk to you."

She lifts her eyes, and I notice she's wearing a little more makeup than she usually does.

Why are you noticing stupid crap like that? Just get a fucking drink, you pussy-deprived idiot.

"Go talk to Joan if you're nervous. She's nice. You'll be fine."

She nods. "Okay, okay. You're right. Not about you being hot, but the other stuff."

I bristle at her teasing for just a moment before I realize it's nothing. I'm just wound too tight for no reason at all.

I hold my hand out toward her, and she peers down at it with a frown before slapping hers to mine and saying, "High five."

I shake my head, laughing. "No. Money me."

"Huh?"

"You're buying tonight." I wiggle my fingers. "Money me."

With a sigh, she reaches into the tiny purse she has slung around her body and pulls her credit card free, slapping it into my hand with a little too much force.

"Barely touch a guy's dick one time and you owe him for life."

"Not for life, just tonight. And once a year after."

She shakes her head. "Go get me a drink before I change my mind and go home."

"You wouldn't dare bail already."

"Want to test me?"

"You don't scare me, Caroline. Now go mingle."

I give her a gentle push toward the table, then slide past her, making sure to keep my distance and not accidentally brush up against her.

Shayla, the woman who's usually behind the bar, spots me from the other end and tells the second bartender she's got this one as I approach.

She sashays over to me, her perky tits barely contained by her tight, small top.

"Hey, handsome," she purrs, leaning across the bar and pressing her breasts together. They're now dangerously close to spilling free.

"Hey, Shay," I say. "How you been?"

"Good, but not as good as I've been before."

I'm not an idiot. I know she's referring to the night we had together when our company first started coming here. It was a one-time thing, and I made sure that was clear when my boss began bringing us here almost every Friday.

Every time I come in, she references our roll in the hay and how nobody else has come close to rocking her world like that. Sad, because all I did was make her come. But I think she's accepted there won't be a repeat.

"Can you start a tab for me?"

"Sure thing. What'll it be tonight, handsome? Your usual?"

I nod. "A spiced rum and root beer too."

She lifts her perfectly sculpted brow. "Two drinks?"

You're here with someone? That's what she's really asking.

"Two drinks tonight."

"Pity." She pouts, and I don't correct her that I'm here with my best friend and not a date. "Be right back."

She flounces away, putting extra sway into her hips. She's hot, I'll give her that, but she's not what I'm after at the moment.

I rest my back against the bar, turning toward the crowd, scanning it for someone to help take me down off this edge I seem to be standing on.

My eyes eventually land back on my co-workers. Paul is chatting with Chad One and Chad Two, two other developers, while the rest of the group seems to be enraptured by a story being told by Drake, our resident class clown.

Joan is talking with another coder, and Caroline is...

Wait. Where the fuck is Caroline?

I push to my full height, scanning the space again.

Damn it's crowded in here.

I'm having a tough time spotting her—but then the distinct color of her dress catches my eye.

She's in the corner of the bar talking with Eli.

Fuck. Of course that tool would defy my direct order. He does it all the time during projects. He's a fucking know-it-all and way too anal about some crap.

Eli is a jackass on a good day, but get a few drinks in him and he's even worse.

He's rowdy. Loud. Brash.

And definitely not fucking good enough for Caroline.

"Here you go, handsome," Shayla says, drawing my attention. "Just let me know when you're ready to close out."

I nod my thanks, grab our drinks, and beeline straight for my best friend and the office tool.

She's smiling, but I know her. It's not *her* smile. It's strained.

She's hating every single second of talking to him, but she's way too polite to tell him otherwise.

"Hey," I say, sliding up to her. She looks at me with relieved eyes. "Got your drink."

"Oh, hey, Bennett." Eli nods, taking a pull off his beer, then wiping his mouth with the back of his hand. "Was just telling your *friend* here about our latest project."

"The one she already knows all about?" I lift my brow. "My *friend* is also my roommate. She's probably more aware of what our project entails than you are some days."

Caroline covers her laugh with her glass, taking a sip from her drink. I try hard not to bash my co-workers because we all have our faults, but she's more than aware of how much Eli irritates the living piss out of me.

Eli's eyes dart between us. "I didn't realize you two were living together."

"Yep. Since when, Care? Freshman year of college?"

"The summer before then," she corrects.

"Right. The summer before."

"I didn't realize you weren't living at home anymore, Bennett. Thought for sure *one* of your *mommies* still made you lunch."

I don't miss the inflection in his voice, and I narrow my eyes at him.

If he thinks making jokes about the fact that I have two mothers is the way to go about getting Caroline's affection, he's an even bigger idiot than I thought.

There are many days I think my moms love my best friend more than me. She's practically a daughter to them, and Caroline will defend their relationship with everything she has if she needs to.

"Oh, man." Caroline practically moans. "I wish Momma Bennett made you lunch. I'd have her make tuna salad at least three times a week."

"I hate tuna salad."

"I know, but I love it. This isn't about you, Coop. Keep up."

"You'd seriously request that *my* mother make a meal I hate just because you like it? Do you think she loves you more than me?"

"Yes. We both know I'm Momma B's favorite, just like we both know you're Momma Kira's favorite. She always wanted a boy."

"That's messed up. They picked *me* from the adoption agency. They both wanted me."

"They picked you because they felt bad for you. You were so ugly that nobody else wanted you. I've seen your baby pictures." She shrugs. "You were a pity adoption."

I scowl at her. "Brat."

She sticks her tongue out playfully, then takes another sip of her drink.

Eli glances between us again, his brows pinched tightly together.

I'm sure he's realizing now how bored Caroline was with their conversation and how, in the few minutes I've been standing here, she's turned into a different person.

Which means he's probably realizing he has absolutely no fucking chance with her.

I pierce him with a stare that says, *Move along, jackass.*

"You know, I think I heard Matt call for me," he says, taking the hint. "It was nice meeting you, Caroline."

"You too, Eli."

He walks away, and I lean down to her. "When I told you to mingle, I didn't mean with him."

"I couldn't run away fast enough when he told me his

name. I recognized it instantly. I know how you feel about him."

"I'm sure he's not a completely bad guy, but fuck does he drive me mad at work."

"He's caused you to break at least two keyboards. That's enough for me to stay far away from him." She presses up on her tiptoes. "See? I'm a good friend too."

Someone bumps into her from behind and she stumbles into me.

On instinct, I wrap my arm around her waist, catching her.

"Hey! Watch it!" I yell at the guy.

He ignores me.

"Fucking jackass," I spit at him, glowering at his back.

"Uh, Coop?"

"Huh?" I pull my gaze to Caroline. "What?"

I realize my arm is still wrapped around her waist and I'm holding her close.

Too close.

I can feel the beat of the music through her body kind of close.

Can feel her hot breath seeping through my shirt.

The curve of her waist that's biting into my fingertips.

If I keep her here for much longer, she'll be able to feel me—all of me—too.

I clear my throat, setting her back onto her feet and putting some space between us.

What is with me tonight? Am I really that deprived of human contact?

With a headshake, I down the full contents of my glass.

I need more.

"Gonna grab another. You good?"

She nods as she studies me with curious eyes.

"Good."

I stalk away before she can study me too much more.

Shayla sees me approaching, and I shake my glass at her.

She sets to work making my usual and I scan the crowd again, this time putting my full concentration on every female who isn't my best friend.

There's a brunette sitting a few tables away who catches my eye.

She smiles, then lifts a daiquiri to her lips. Ugh. No. She'll taste like sugar after drinking that.

I give her a tight smile and then move on.

There's a redhead toward the end of the bar, her fingers playing with the straw in her drink as she stares out at the crowd.

She's hot, her bright yellow top making her hair stand out, and I can see a bit of ink poking out on her back where shirt and jeans don't quite meet.

Well, hello there.

I grab my drink from Shayla and take a step toward her. I don't make it a whole foot before a girl slides up next to her, placing a kiss on her cheek. They embrace, then start making out hardcore in the middle of the bar.

Aaand never mind.

I return to my perch, moving on through the crowd.

Too available. Too not available.

Too drunk. Too loud. Crying.

Nobody is standing out…until red catches my gaze.

Caroline.

Color me fucking shocked.

She's out on the dance floor…and she's not alone.

There's a guy with his hand on her waist in a way that seems proper but somehow feels way too fucking intimate all at the same time.

He dips his head toward her and says something in her ear, and she tosses her head back, laughing at whatever he says.

A surge of anger rushes through me seeing her laugh like that.

I hate myself for it instantly.

I don't understand what my problem is. She's my best friend. That's it.

I do not and never have harbored feelings for her, because that one week during the summer between our freshman and sophomore year of high school doesn't count.

Am I really going to let one absurd and not-likely-to-ever-happen-again incident like her seeing me naked change our entire friendship?

No.

That'd be dumb.

But…I did like the way she looked at me.

And I can't stop thinking about how much I want her to look at me like that again.

Not just some girl either.

Her.

I want my best friend to look at me like she wants me.

Because…*fuck me.*

I think I want her.

Chapter 6

CAROLINE

I NOW UNDERSTAND how Cooper felt last night when I got a full look at him in the hallway.

Sure, I might not have been naked in front of him earlier, but I felt completely bare.

The way his eyes lingered on me when I walked out of my bedroom in my new design has been burned into my skin all night long.

Even now, dancing with this incredibly hot guy who has made me laugh with his silly pickup line, I can feel it still.

It feels like he etched his name into my flesh and marked me for life.

Calvin, my dance partner, points toward the bar.

I nod, needing another drink to help keep my mind clear of Cooper and his stare.

He clasps my hand in his and pulls me through the crowd.

I try hard not to think about how his hand feels compared to Cooper's. They're not the same, that's for sure.

Ugh. Stop thinking about him.

We squeeze into a spot at the bar, and he motions for the bartender.

A beautiful blonde with boobs that'd make any girl jealous saunters up to us.

"What can I get for you two?"

"Whatever bottle you have on special," he tells her before looking at me expectantly.

It takes me a second to realize why he's staring at me.

He wants my drink order.

It's weird. I can't remember the last time I had to tell someone what I want. Cooper always knows exactly what to order me.

"My treat," he pushes.

I don't tell him I already have a tab here. Who doesn't like free drinks?

"A spiced rum and root beer, please," I say to the bartender.

She tilts her head, studying me with pursed lips.

"What?" I ask.

"Nothing." She shakes her head. "I'll be right back with your drinks."

I don't have a second to think about it as Calvin dances his fingers along my arm, drawing my attention.

"So," he says, grinning down at me, "what's your thing?"

I scrunch my brows together. "My thing?"

"Yeah, like what do you do?"

"For an occupation?"

"Sure. Or a hobby."

I don't share my hobby with anyone. In fact, the only people who know I design are Cooper, River, and our other business partner, Maya.

That's it.

Not even my dad knows I make my own clothes. He still complains every time I talk to him, saying I'm squandering my college degree by working in a "second-rate store," as he calls it.

"I work at a popular boutique over on Second Street. Maybe you've heard of it. Making Waves?"

He nods. "Oh yeah. My ex-girlfriend loved that place. I've dropped a lot of money in there. You're welcome."

He laughs, and I smile politely, not really liking his joke, like he's solely responsible for my salary or something.

But maybe I'm just being sensitive and perhaps a tad picky.

"I'm a real estate agent," he provides. "Business around here is booming with the legalization of marijuana. All those potheads moving here in droves, and I'm the one reaping the benefits."

Making so much money he's ordering the cheapest beer on the menu?

He's either cheap or full of shit.

You're not here to fall in love, Caroline, just to get laid. He's hot—stop nitpicking.

"What a lucky business to be in, then," I tell him.

"Here are those drinks." The bartender slides our order across the bar.

"Thanks," Calvin says, handing over his credit card, chugging half his beer in one go.

I take a healthy drink of my cocktail, thirsty from being on the dance floor.

"Good?" he asks, like he's the one who made it. "Another? The drinks are good here but tiny. Plus, I'm sure you're warm in that outfit of yours." He pulls his lips between his teeth, raking his eyes over my body. "Though damn is it hot on you."

I blush. I am a little warm in my sweater dress. I didn't think there'd be so many people here tonight when I planned the outfit, but then I don't ever go out. How was I supposed to know?

"Sure, I'll take another," I tell him. "Thank you."

"No problem."

He calls the bartender over again, ordering another round of our drinks.

"That's an odd drink order," he says when she walks away. "Haven't heard that one before."

"Really? You've never had spiced rum and root beer together? It's so good, even better when you add a splash of Irish cream to it."

He wrinkles his nose. "Not a big hard liquor fan. Would much rather have a good, local IPA."

"I'm not a big beer fan."

"You're missing out. There are so many good local breweries you could be visiting." He downs the rest of his first beer just as the bartender slips our second round across the bar top. "You from around here?"

"Sort of," I tell him. "I'm originally from Florida. My best friend and I moved here for college and decided we liked it, so we stayed. We've been here about seven years now."

"You chose to stay in Colorado over going back to Florida? The Sunshine State for all this craptastic weather? You're nuts, girl." He shakes his head. "Beautiful, but nuts."

I lift a shoulder. "Trust me, you get tired of nothing but sunshine and hurricanes after a while. Besides, Cooper got an excellent job here right after graduation. It just made sense to stay."

"Cooper? Your boyfriend?"

I shake my head. "No. The best friend I came here to go to college with."

"Your best friend is a guy?"

"Um…yes?"

I don't know why it comes out as a question, but I guess that's because I don't understand why he's questioning my friendship.

"And that works for you?"

"Being friends? Yes."

He shakes his head, taking another drink from his beer. "No—being friends with a guy."

"Oh. That." I nod. "Yeah, it works for us."

"You don't have feelings for him you're hung up on or anything? Haven't been secretly in love with him since you were kids or something?"

Since we were kids? When he was a lanky, overconfident jock who thought he was God's gift to women even though he could barely speak to them? The one who was so sick one time he shit his pants from coughing so hard? That same guy?

No. I am *not* secretly in love with Cooper.

I wrinkle my nose. "Heavens no. We're just friends. I've known him way too long to be in love with him."

"No repressed sexual desires, then?"

I gulp.

Not until recently. Not until I saw exactly the kind of man that same lanky kid grew up to be.

I force a laugh, hoping it doesn't come out sounding too

fake. "No. Nothing like that. We've been friends since we were fifteen. I've been there through *all* his awkward teen years, including when he thought it was cool to dress in those god-awful cargo shorts. That's enough to scar me for life." I finish off my first drink and reach for my second. "We're just friends."

"Good." A grin stretches across his face. I'm sure he thinks he looks sexy and confident, and he has the confident part right, but it's definitely not in a good way. He appears a little too sure of himself. "Glad to hear that."

"So, do you—"

"Do you—"

We laugh when we speak at the same time.

I motion for him to go first.

"Do you sing? Want to try out the karaoke? They should be starting soon."

Man, if Cooper were here, he'd laugh until he was red in the face because he knows damn well I'd rather step on a Lego than sing karaoke.

I crinkle my nose. "I have had nowhere near enough alcohol for that."

"Aw, come on. You shy, babe?"

"Something like that."

He nods. "That's all right. We'll get a few more drinks in you and you'll be singing in no time."

Highly doubt that.

"What about dancing? Want to do that again?"

"Sure," I agree.

It's not my favorite, but it sounds a hell of a lot better than karaoke.

I finish off my drink, instantly regretting slamming it

when my cheeks grow hotter as the alcohol hits my system. "Lead the way."

Calvin grabs my hand again and pulls me back out onto the floor.

He puts one hand on my waist and uses the other to take long pulls off his beer.

We move to the music as best we can, but we're completely out of sync.

Maybe it's him, maybe it's the booze in my system, but I'm thankful when he motions toward the bar two songs later.

I shake my head. "I'm good, but you can go grab one."

"You'll be here when I get back?" he asks, dragging his teeth over his bottom lip.

I bet he thinks he looks sexy, but it just looks awkward on him.

A giggle bubbles free because all I can picture is that time Cooper was making fun of my teen drama shows and all the lip-biting they do by biting his top lip instead of his bottom. He walked around doing it at the most embarrassing times for a week.

Maybe I'm tipsier than I thought.

He laughs at me giggling uncontrollably, shaking his head. "Don't disappear on me, babe."

Then he's gone, pushing through the crowd toward the bar.

Babe. I try not to roll my eyes at the pet name, a sure sign he doesn't remember my name at all.

I'm not usually one to dance unless I have a lot of alcohol in my system, but when Calvin asked and batted his amber eyes at me, I couldn't say no.

Besides, tonight is supposed to be about trying new things, right?

Now that I'm here, I don't want to leave.

It kind of feels nice to disappear into the crowd. Sitting on the outskirts almost feels more terrifying. I'm much more the focus of others' attention, more approachable.

In here, it's all limbs and rhythm and freedom.

Geez. I know I don't drink often, but man am I feeling it tonight. How strong do they make the drinks here? Eh, whatever. I could use a night of fun.

I let myself relax into the music, swaying with the beat and getting lost in the loud bass.

Cooper was right—they do play their music too loud, but I don't hate it. It's distracting, and I could use a distraction right now.

Anything to help me not think about the fact that Cooper looked at me like he never has before.

And the fact that I liked it.

A lot.

Like so much I want him to look at me like that again.

Just keep dancing and keep distracting yourself. Stop thinking about Cooper. Tonight is about fun. It's about relaxing. Tonight is about getting laid. Nothing else. Nobody else.

I move to the music, dancing through another song by myself, and then I start to wonder if Calvin is going to return.

I dance my way closer to the bar, trying to get a glimpse and see if I can spot him.

He's there all right.

Lips locked tightly with someone else.

So much for that.

Oh well. He wasn't that great of a dancer anyway and kind of gave off douchebag vibes. A little too full of himself for my liking.

I'm about to turn back into the crowd when a nagging stops me in my tracks, like I'm being watched.

I slide my eyes toward the other end of the bar.

There he is.

Watching me.

Cooper's light green eyes are locked on me like I'm the only person in the room. The hair on my arms stands on end, and I shiver.

Lust.

Even from here, it's clear as day.

Cooper is staring at me like he wants to eat me alive.

He tips his glass of whiskey to his lips, taking a long sip, not once moving his eyes off me.

It's intoxicating and nerve-racking all at once.

The nerves win, and I flee back onto the dance floor, hiding from his scrutiny. Hiding from the thoughts I shouldn't be having that are swimming in my head.

It's too much at once, and I need a second away from him.

Not once in the last ten years of friendship have I had anything other than platonic thoughts about Cooper.

Now I can't seem to stop thinking about him in very *non*platonic ways.

Two hands curl around my waist, and for a split second, I panic.

Then the familiar scent washes over me.

Sage.

Warm.

Summer nights.

Cooper.

His fingers dig into my hips, pulling me into him until my back is flush with his front.

As if we've done this a thousand times before—and we certainly haven't, not even once—he takes control, moving us in perfect sync.

His chest is hard, his arms strong.

He feels like Cooper and a stranger all at the same time.

The song ends and another begins.

We don't stop dancing.

Cooper's grip tightens, almost to the point of hurting, but I don't dare try to move, not wanting to break this spell we seem to be under.

I like it too much.

The alcohol.

It has to be that hindering my inhibitions.

These feelings aren't real. They're booze-infused.

That's why I don't move when his lips ghost along my throat.

It's why I lean into his touch.

Why I spin in his arms and wrap my own around his neck.

And it's the culprit for every stupid action I take.

Like pressing up onto my tiptoes and bringing my mouth just inches from his. Threading my fingers through his always-messy-in-that-effortless-way hair. Pulling him closer.

His burning stare bores into me, hotter than anything I've ever felt before. The sweat dripping down my neck isn't from the dancing or the crowd.

It's from him.

I press into him. So close I can feel his chest brushing against mine.

Close enough that if anyone were to bump into us right now, our lips would instantly collide.

"Caroline…" he whispers, his lips grazing mine just enough to make me yearn for more, his hand crashing into my hair and holding me still. "What's happening here?"

I peel my eyes open and meet his hungry gaze.

And just like that, the spell is broken.

I push out of his arms, putting much-needed space between us.

Oh hell. What is *happening here? What the hell are we doing?*

I cover my mouth with my hand, shaking my head.

Then, I run.

"Caroline!" I hear him call after me.

I don't look back.

I don't stop running until I'm in the hallway leading to the bathrooms.

Even back here, there are bodies, but at least it's not as crowded, making it a bit easier to breathe.

And a breath is exactly what I need right now.

I press my back against the wall, the cool touch of the wood just what I need to calm my erratic heartbeat.

I close my eyes, sucking in gulps of air, trying to get a sense of what the hell I was thinking almost letting Cooper kiss me.

Well, technically, I almost kissed him too.

Have I seriously had so much to drink tonight I'm that unaware of what I'm doing?

You wanted him to kiss you.

Another deep breath. A long exhale.

Repeat, repeat, repeat.

Just when I think I have my shit together, I feel him.

My eyes flutter open, and there he stands. Just out of reach. Staring at me with those hungry eyes again.

I brush my tongue over my lips, my mouth suddenly dry.

He tracks the movement with his gaze, swallowing roughly, throat bobbing.

Then, he takes a slow step toward me.

And another.

I don't move.

Not when he reaches out and slips his fingers over my hips.

Not when he steps closer, fitting himself against me like he's done it before.

And not even when he leans forward, running his nose along my jawline up to my ear.

He pauses. And we're back to not moving.

I can feel his chest brushing against mine, can feel how hard his heart is beating. Mine is doing the same.

I don't know how long we stay like this. How many songs pass, how many bodies move around us. How many times his fingers tighten and loosen on my waist, like he's fighting with himself to do something or walk away.

I'm fighting too.

Someone jostles us and he's forced to close that last gap of space between us.

I feel him.

Everywhere.

"Fuck," I hear him mutter quietly.

It comes out somewhere between a curse and a plea.

I don't know who moves first, but suddenly our mouths are fused together.

Cooper Bennett is kissing me, and I kiss him back.

I twine my arms around his neck, driving my fingers through his hair, pulling at the ends. Pulling him closer.

His mouth moves against mine like he was made for kissing me. His tongue darts out to slide across the seam of my lips, wasting no time. He pushes inside my mouth, kissing me expertly.

And I guess he is an expert. His experience is much greater than mine has ever been.

Is this seriously what I've been missing out on? Kisses like this?

His hands hold my hips tightly, pulling me in. Holding me close like he's scared if he lets go even just a bit, I'll run. Scared I'll come right back down to earth and realize this is the worst idea ever.

Oh shit. What am I doing?

Like he can read my thoughts, Cooper wrenches his mouth from mine, and we both gasp for air.

He peers down at me, eyes hazy and filled with a combination of desire and confusion.

What the hell are we thinking?

We aren't—that's the problem.

We're not thinking. We're just acting.

And we're ruining everything.

His brows crease together. His features crumple at the realization of what we just did.

"Caroline…"

I shake my head. "No."

I shove past him.

This time, he doesn't follow.

Chapter 7

COOPER

AS SOON AS I got a grip on myself after the world's worst moment of weakness, I went in search of Caroline.

I couldn't find her anywhere.

Not even Shayla had seen her to close out her tab.

Just when I was about to head outside and run down the streets looking for her, my phone buzzed in my pocket.

Caroline: I'm fine. In an Uber.

Caroline: We'll talk tomorrow.

Except that was three days ago and we still haven't spoken a word to each other.

I didn't even bother drinking myself into a stupor after she left the bar. I closed our tab, told the guys good night, and took the long way home.

I don't know how long I walked out in the cold alone, but no matter how long it was, it wasn't enough to cool myself off from our kiss.

When I got home, her door was closed.

And it's stayed that way since.

I got up early Saturday morning to talk with her, but she was already gone, a pot of fresh coffee in the brewer.

It's as close to talking as we've come.

It's Monday night, and even though she's been home all day too, we've stayed in our own areas of the apartment.

I can hear her now. She's sitting in the living room watching her TV show, giggling at something they're saying.

I'm holed up in my room because it's better than being out there with her.

How do I explain what the fuck I was thinking when I kissed her? When I danced with her? Hell, when I was looking at her like I was?

I'm scared to face her. Terrified to face what happened.

Afraid to face the reality that maybe friends isn't all I want to be.

Fuck. I wish I had someone else to talk to about this. But no, I had to go and screw things up with the one person I'd normally be going to with my problems.

An email from work pops up in the corner of my computer screen.

I ignore it. I worked my ass off all weekend. I deserve a break.

Plus, it's past five, so I'm technically off the clock.

Off the clock and fucking starving. My stomach growls for the fifth time in as many minutes.

I haven't eaten since breakfast this morning when I had the place to myself. The egg whites I had are long since digested. I need food.

Now.

There's a soft knock on my door, and my heart starts beating double time.

Caroline pushes my bedroom door open with more hesitation than she's ever used, and that includes after she swore she caught me with a boner (she did) looking at porn (I was).

She stands just outside my room in a matching set of pajamas that have little books scattered all over them.

I almost laugh because that's just who she is when it comes to her pajamas: either matching perfectly or not at all.

Her contacts out, the oversized glasses she hardly ever wears adorably cover her face. Her blonde hair that I now know feels just like what I imagine heaven to feel like is piled on top of her head in one of those intentionally messy buns girls like to wear.

One sock-clad foot is sitting atop the other as she fingers the ragged edges of her sleep top.

She looks as nervous as I feel.

I clear my throat. "What's up?"

"Uh, hey," she says quietly, not quite avoiding looking at me but not making eye contact either. "I was thinking about ordering some pizza and watching a movie. I wanted to know if you want to join me."

I lift a brow. "Do you want me to join you?"

Her face twists. "Well, I am asking for a reason."

Her eyes say, *I miss my best friend.*

And, fuck, I miss mine too.

"Then yes, I'm down for a movie and pizza night."

"Good. Why don't you order the pizza and I'll pick out the movie?"

I laugh and push out of my chair. "Nice try. *I'll* pick the movie, you order. I do not feel like watching some cheesy rom-com tonight."

"I'm not really in the mood for romance right now." Her cheeks go pink. "Kind of burned out on it."

Meaning she doesn't want to watch a romantic movie with me.

I get it. I do. Probably not the best idea right now anyway.

"Right." I nod. "Even better. I can pick a movie that definitely doesn't have any romance in it, then."

I walk toward her, and she practically trips over her own feet to keep a safe distance between us.

I try not to let her see how much it bothers me.

"Nothing too scary," she requests as I follow her down the hall. "And nothing too violent."

"That's not leaving me a lot of options."

"I don't know about you, but a comedy sounds good to me," she says, bending over at the table we have next to the door, fishing around inside her purse.

My eyes fall straight to her ass and the tiny shorts she's wearing.

Look away, Cooper. This is the kind of shit that got you in trouble last time. Look what that led to.

She stands and I dart my eyes anywhere but at her, hoping she didn't just catch me staring.

She shoves her card at me. "Here. I'll buy."

"No," I tell her, pushing it back her way. "You got breakfast and drinks the other night. It's my turn."

Just like that, the air between us shifts, the mention of the other night hanging over us like a thick cloud.

We don't move, her hand still outstretched, holding on to her card from one end while I hold on from the other.

I could easily pull her to me. Could wrap my arm around her waist and haul her onto her tiptoes until her mouth is even with mine. Could press our lips together and revel in how good she feels again.

But I shouldn't. I fucking shouldn't and I *know* I shouldn't.

I shouldn't want to kiss my best friend.

I clear my throat, letting go of the card. "Seriously, Care, I got it."

She nods, then tucks the card back into her purse.

"What do you want on the pizza?" she asks, grabbing her phone and scrolling to find the place we always order from. "The usual?"

"Extra black olives."

"Ew." She scrunches her nose, bringing the phone up to her ear.

"Pretty sure you can't say ew when you eat *pineapple* on your half."

"I can and will say ew because *ew*. Also, since you're buying, I'm ordering breadsticks."

"Mooch."

"Cheap ass." She flips me off. "Hi, yes," she says in her sweetest voice, "I'd like to place an order for delivery, please."

She moves into the kitchen to rattle off our order and grab drinks.

We'll spend the time it takes them to deliver the pizza watching previews and deciding on a movie. When Caroline said it was my turn to pick, she meant the genre. After that's decided, we still must agree on the actual movie we'll watch.

It's our routine, and it feels good to be doing something normal.

After tossing some money on the table, I grab the remote

and settle onto the couch in my spot, navigating back to the home screen of the movie app.

"Here," she says, handing me a can of flavored carbonated water. "We ran out of lime."

"Thanks," I say, popping the top and taking a hefty swig.

Ugh. Grapefruit. My least favorite.

Caroline settles onto the couch, tucking her legs beneath her. It doesn't escape my notice that she's sitting on the complete opposite end of the couch, as far away from me as she can possibly get.

Guess I spoke too soon about normal.

Usually, she'll come in here and grab her blanket, then lay her head on my lap, where she'll inevitably fall asleep once her belly is full.

Not anymore.

We ruined that.

She pops the top on her own drink and takes a sip.

I catch the color of the can from the corner of my eye.

"I thought you said we ran out of lime."

"We did. Just now." She shrugs, taking another drink.

"And I thought you were a good friend."

Do good friends kiss each other?

"I *am* a good friend. Case in point: I didn't stop being your friend when you told the entire ninth grade class I had mono from practicing kissing on the water fountain."

"I totally saw you using tongue on that thing."

She rolls her eyes. "Just start scrolling."

I navigate to the comedy section and flip through the movies until something jumps out at me.

I pause on one and we watch the preview.

A light chuckle from her, nothing from me.

Pass.

We do it again. Then again. And at least five more times.

Until finally we settle on something that gets more than a chuckle from both of us.

Just as we've decided on a movie, the doorbell rings.

"I'll get it!"

She bounces from her seat, running toward the door like she's starving.

I watch her talk to the delivery guy.

I watch him scroll his eyes down her body and stare at her for far too fucking long.

I clench my jaw tightly, trying to resist the urge to do something dumb like walk over there and put my arm around her waist.

Like she's fucking mine or something.

I sit here stoically as it takes way longer than it should to get the pizza, doing everything I can to not listen in on their conversation.

When she finally closes the door, I snap my attention back to the TV, even though nothing is playing yet.

"You are never going to believe who that was."

"Who?" I play along.

"Remember that guy from the bookstore who's always in there when I am?"

"The stalker who wants to bang you?"

She huffs. "He is not a stalker. It's just a coincidence that we ran into him at The Gravy Train too."

"Yeah, he's just *coincidentally* stalking you."

"Anyway," she says, setting the pizza down on the coffee table and resuming her spot. She slides a couple napkins my way, then leans forward, popping the top of the delicious-smelling pie and grabbing a slice. "He delivers pizza at night now to cover his book-spending habit."

I snort, reaching for my own piece. "Sounds like a nerd."

"And when he saw my name come up on the queue," she continues, ignoring me, "he took a chance and grabbed the order."

I pause my pizza slice halfway to my mouth, looking over at her. "He knows your name?"

"Yeah?" She shrugs. "I go to the bookstore a lot."

I put the slice back down. "I don't know, Caroline...I don't like that he just happened to show up at the apartment."

"He didn't just *show up*. I ordered pizza. He was working. He delivered it." She takes a bite of her pizza, chews, then wipes at her mouth with her napkin.

"Come on. You say this guy is at the bookstore every time you're there. Now suddenly he conveniently works at our favorite pizza place we order from all the time?" I shake my head, biting off half my slice. "Sounds fishy."

"You're overreacting. Anyway, he just asked me if I wanted to get drinks with him on Wednesday. I said yes."

"You said *yes*?"

"Why are you making such a big deal out of this?"

"I'm not."

"Yes, you are. Look, I'm used to your territorial tendencies, but *you're* the one who said it was a good idea to get me laid and offered to help. *This* isn't helping."

That was before we kissed and it rocked my fucking world.

"Is this about the other night?"

Splat.

My pizza slips right from my fingers, smacking loudly

against the hardwood floor, just catching the edge of the blue and gray rug we have under the table.

Thank fuck we don't have carpet.

"Cooper!" She shoots off the couch, grabbing for napkins.

"What?" It comes out as a growl as I push to my feet, shoving the coffee table out of the way to clean the mess up.

"You got sauce on the rug. I'm going to have to scrub it now."

"It's not like I fucking threw it on the floor! It's greasy and slipped."

I stomp into the kitchen to grab a wet towel, annoyed.

At myself for dropping the pizza.

At her for saying yes to a date with some idiot after what happened between us.

And then again at myself for even caring about the kiss.

I grab a hand towel, wet it under the faucet, and make my way back out to the living room.

Caroline's on her hands and knees cleaning up the mess I made.

Her pert ass is in the air, almost sticking out of the bottom of her pajamas that are getting to be way too small for her.

It's like she's trying to fucking kill me.

"Can't believe you dropped your pizza. First, that's rude because it's *pizza*. Second, now I'll probably have to steam clean the rug." She looks at me over her shoulder. "Oh, good. You got a towel."

I don't move.

I can't.

If I move, I'll do something stupid like pick her up and carry her to my bedroom.

She looks like a wet fucking dream right now, and it's taking everything I have not to act on my impulses.

"Hello." She holds her hand out. "Towel, please."

"Get up."

Her brows pinch together. "Huh?"

"Get. Up."

She groans, pushing herself to her feet. "Ugh, bossy much?"

I shove past her, dropping in front of her to finish cleaning up the mess.

It's a bad idea.

A bad, *bad* idea.

Her knees are red from pressing against the hardwood.

The only time I want to see her knees red is when she's on them for me.

The thought slams into me, and I try to block out the images that come along with it.

"Seriously, what is your damage? First you're being a jerk about the first guy who is actually interested in dating me in I don't know how long. Now you're being one because *you* dropped pizza on the floor. I don't even understand what's up with you tonight. It's like—"

Her words die on her tongue.

Because my hand is now wrapped around her right ankle.

She inhales a sharp breath, and I dare a peek up at her.

She's staring down at me with cautious eyes.

Cautious eyes that are filled with an ache.

Not dropping eye contact, I drag my hand higher, ghosting my fingers up her calf.

When I stop at her knee, she's barely breathing.

I run my fingertips over the redness, hating to see her

marked up because of my stupid mistake. I don't know what possesses me to do it, but I lean forward and press a gentle kiss to the spot.

Soft. That's how her skin feels.

Just like her lips, which are now parted on a sweet sigh, felt.

She swallows thickly, eyes darkening.

Feeling brave, I kiss her again, this time just half an inch higher.

Another sigh.

Another kiss.

And another.

My lips brush her barely there shorts, and I'm fairly sure she's not even breathing at all anymore.

I'm not sure I am either.

"Cooper…"

I swallow, my lips brushing against her leg with the movement.

"We should go to bed."

I look up at her, and her face flushes with embarrassment. "Not together," she rushes out. "*Separately.*"

With a whole lot of willpower, I pull away from her and tilt my head back.

"About Friday…" She darts her tongue out to wet her lips, and I remember just how good that same tongue felt against my own just three nights ago. "We can't."

Two words.

Whispered.

Yet so fucking loud.

She doesn't want this.

She doesn't want me.

I push to my full height, putting distance between us because I really fucking need it.

She stands there, wringing her hands together, lip tucked between her teeth.

"It's just...we're best friends, you know? We can't go there. It's just not something you can come back from."

She's right. I know she's right.

Doesn't mean I want her to be right.

I want her to be anything *but* right.

"You understand, don't you? Friday was just a fluke. We were drunk."

I was sober.

She's a lightweight, but not *that* big of one.

And it wasn't just a fluke.

At least I don't think it was.

But maybe I've read this all wrong. Maybe she hasn't been feeling anything happening between us. Maybe I'm just a moron and almost screwed everything up just like I tried to do when we were teens and I kissed her.

We're perfect as friends.

No reason to screw that up, right?

"Right." I clear my throat when the word comes out hoarse. "You're right. It was just a one-off thing. A mistake. It won't happen again."

"Because we'd be fools to ruin this great friendship we have."

"Exactly," I agree.

"Besides, I know you slept with a teddy bear until you were twenty-one. That's not something you should know about someone you're sleeping with."

"True." I laugh lightly. "You know what happens if you ever tell anyone about that, right?"

"You'll post pictures of me with my underwear on my head on the internet, from that time I was super drunk."

I nod. "Precisely."

"Even though that's totally not a fair playing field. I was drunk—you knew exactly what you were doing."

"I'll deny it until I die."

She grins, shaking her head at me. She looks down at the mess on the floor, then drops her head back on a groan. "Ugh. I really hate steam cleaning too."

"I'll worry about cleaning the rug. Tomorrow. Tonight, let's just watch a movie, huh?"

"You still want to watch a movie?"

"Yeah. We've kind of been ignoring each other for the last few days. And, well, you better not tell anyone this, but I sort of missed you."

She laughs. "I sort of missed you too."

She peeks up, her blue eyes studying me probably harder than they ever have.

I will myself not to react. Will myself to remain cool. Neutral. To not let her know there's a whole shitstorm of emotions whirling inside.

Sadness. Regret. Confusion.

Disappointment.

"Are we good?" she asks.

"Of course. Come on. I'm fucking starving."

Chapter 8

CAROLINE

WE CAN'T.

Those two words have been haunting me for days now.

For the most part, things with Cooper have gone back to normal. Or as normal as things can be between two best friends who kissed.

It's as if there's a thin cloud of uncertainty just floating above us, waiting to crack open and shake everything up again.

Part of me wanted to tell Cooper to keep going, wanted to see how far we'd take it.

But the other, more logical part of my brain said to stop.

Crossing that line would be a bad idea. He's too important to me to lose over something like sex. I don't want to risk my friendship with him all for a good lay.

And I know it would be a good lay too.

If Cooper can fuck half as good as he can kiss...

"Earth to Caroline." River waves her hand in front of my face. "Company meeting here."

I give myself a shake, dragging my attention back to the task at hand.

It's Wednesday morning and we're discussing the big event we have in a month.

Every year our community throws the Harristown Jubilee, a big gathering of food trucks, music, and whatever else anyone wants to sell. Homemade pastries, home goods, clothes—anything goes. The event is huge, and sellers tend to make their booth fees back within the hour, not to mention the foot traffic and getting your name out there is priceless.

I should probably be paying attention since we'll all be there running the food truck we turned into the mobile closet this year.

"Sorry," I say. "I'm listening."

A frown pulls at her lips. "You okay?"

"Fine, fine." I nod, waving off her concern, reaching across the counter for the coffees she brought us. "Just didn't sleep well last night is all. I'm tired. Not that I have to tell you about that."

River has insomnia and has come to work on little sleep many times over the last few years.

Luckily, with her new relationship with Dean, she seems to be taking more time off work and not letting the stress get to her as much. It's doing wonders for her disorder.

"You look like you're a million miles away, not tired. This isn't just company talk time. It's girl talk time too. What's going on?" asks Maya, our other partner, tossing her long chocolate-colored hair over her shoulder.

Maya and River have been best friends since they were little and have been through *everything* together, including Maya's teenage pregnancy and her recent divorce.

They're more like sisters than they are friends.

"Yeah, talk to us," River urges. "Something going on with Cooper?"

I try not to react. Try not to let on that something happened between us.

I tuck a hair behind my ear. "No. Cooper's fine. We're fine."

"Liar!" Maya shouts, pointing at me. "She's a liar! Did you see it?"

"I saw it," River says, nodding.

"Saw what?"

"You tucked your hair behind your ear—it's your tell. You're hiding something."

"I'm not hiding anything," I tell Maya. "There's nothing to hide. And I do not have a tell."

"Uh-huh. This explains why you've been walking around here like a zombie since last Friday. Something definitely happened and you're not fooling us."

"Oh my gosh." River gasps. "Did you finally get laid?"

"What?"

"On your night out with Cooper," she continues. "Did you meet some hot guy and finally get some action?"

Oh. *That.*

Did I get laid? No.

Did I have the best kiss I've ever had? Yes.

Can I *still* feel my lips tingling? Still feel his mouth ghosting up my leg? Double yes.

Do I wish I would have had the courage to tell Cooper to keep going instead of to stop? *Yes.*

"No, I didn't get laid." I take a sip from my coffee. "But I do have a date tonight."

Despite Cooper's warning that it won't work and it's not a smart idea, I haven't canceled my date with Jason. We're supposed to meet for drinks tonight at nine.

There's a nagging feeling in my gut telling me not to go, but I want to do everything I can to put what happened with Cooper out of my mind and move on.

Going out with Jason would be moving on.

I should go…right?

"With whom?"

"Remember a few months ago when I told you about that guy I kept running into at the bookstore?" They both nod. "It's him. We happened upon one another the other day and he finally asked."

"Oh," River says.

They exchange a look but don't say anything.

I have a best friend. I know *exactly* what that look means.

"What?" I ask.

"It's nothing," Maya says with a shrug.

I lift a brow at her.

She sighs. "It's just…well…we thought—"

"That you and Cooper were going to get together," River finishes for her.

Now it's my turn to sigh.

"Guys…" I draw the word out. "Cooper and I…"

"Are perfect for each other," Maya supplies, her best friend bobbing her head in agreement. "Everyone knows the best couples start out as friends."

"Or enemies," River interjects.

"Please." Maya rolls her alluring gray eyes. "You and Dean were never enemies, just idiots who wanted to bump uglies and were too chicken to say so." She turns her attention to me. "You do have feelings for him, don't you?"

"No!"

It comes out quickly.

Too quickly.

They exchange another glance.

I huff. "I mean, I don't know. I *didn't*. Not until…"

"Until what?" River prompts. "Did something happen? Other than you seeing him naked, I mean."

I nod and hate that my cheeks heat at the thought of seeing Cooper naked.

Hate that the ache that's seemed to assume a permanent place between my thighs pulses to let me know it's still there.

"We…uh…we kind of kissed."

"*Kind of* kissed? Or full-on tongue-fucked each other?"

"River!" Maya scolds, laughing at her crassness. "Can't you see the poor girl is already dying of embarrassment? Do you have to be so…you?"

River ignores her. "Was it Friday when you two went out?"

Another nod.

"Ha!" She snaps her fingers together. "I knew it! I knew something was brewing there."

"No you didn't."

"Did too. There was something different about you two at the diner, something that wasn't there before."

"I'd just seen him naked for the first time—that's going to change some things."

She shakes her head, her long red waves bouncing with the movement. "No. It was something else—something more. There was this *electricity*."

"Man, I am so mad I missed that."

"Blame that lazy freakin' kid of yours for sleeping in *again* and missing breakfast," River tells Maya. "All he does is sleep these days."

"It's a teenager thing," Maya says. "Or at least that's what all my parenting blogs tell me. He'll outgrow it. Then he'll get real nasty and mean. Then he'll move out and be the government's problem."

She says it so nonchalantly, but I know she's not serious.

Maya's son, Sam, is her lifeline. She loves that kid more than anything. He's been a bit of a handful lately, in that apathetic teen stage, and he's driving her nuts. She might joke about wishing away the years until he turns eighteen, but I know she doesn't want that to happen fast at all.

"There was no 'electricity,'" I tell River. "You were imagining things."

"Then tell me, oh wise one: if no sparks were flying about, why'd you two kiss that night, huh?"

"I was drunk."

"Bull," she counters quickly. "You're not the type to get shit-faced in public."

That's true. It's not my style.

In fact, the last time I did get drunk was documented by Cooper in those embarrassing photos he has of me, and that was back in college.

But if I tell myself it was just the alcohol that made me let my guard down and give in to the urges I've been having, it'll make the truth a whole lot less real.

I think I might have feelings for Cooper.

And I don't think they're just *in the pants* feelings.

Feelings feelings.

I've been replaying the events of last week in my head, trying to skip over the sexy bits and focusing on all the other pieces.

The in-between moments.

The one where, after our hallway encounter, Cooper came to my room to make sure I was okay. *He* was the one who was violated, and he wanted to make sure *I* was okay.

The moment when he swapped my coffee for his water at The Gravy Train because he knows I try not to drink too much caffeine. When he saw that I was on the verge of a panic attack at the bar and literally held my hand through the whole thing.

And when, after I told him to stop, he stopped instantly. Accepted the boundary I set. Then sat on the couch and watched whatever movie I wanted.

Those small moments.

They're the ones that are making me second-guess myself. They're the ones that make me think taking things to a different level isn't so crazy after all.

But I'm not sure I'm willing to find out which part of me is right.

The logical one that says it'll ruin our friendship, or the one that says I need to try?

Taking that plunge with Cooper is dangerous and unknown, and I like what we have now. Why mess that up based on feelings I *think* I *might* have?

"Personally, I think you should jump on that dick and ride it all night long."

My mouth drops open at Maya's words.

River shakes her head at her friend's outburst. "And you thought what *I* said was bad."

"I'm horny and dick-deprived." Maya shrugs. "Sorry."

"Henry Cavill not cutting it?"

"Oh, trust me—Henry Cavill *always* cuts it. I'm just missing an actual penis. The rubber one kind of gets old after a while."

"But the rubber one doesn't talk back," River says.

"And won't knock you up," I add.

"Wow. You two just made me feel so much better about having a lonely vagina."

We all laugh.

"Okay, I have to ask..." River starts when we all calm back down. "Was he a good kisser? Because he just *looks* like a good kisser."

"How does someone *look* like a good kisser?"

"Trust us—it's a thing," Maya answers. "Stop avoiding the question. Did he, as my best friend so eloquently put it, *tongue-fuck* you?"

Is that what he did when he pressed me against the wall, curled his fingers around my waist, and pressed his mouth to mine like he was born to kiss me?

Yes.

"Oooh. She's blushing," River says excitedly, bouncing her brows up and down. "That's totally a yes."

"It's a yes," I admit quietly. "He's a really good kisser."

A really, *really* good kisser...who I want to kiss again.

"I knew he would be. He has those kissable lips," Maya says.

A spark of jealousy rushes through me at the thought of her ever tasting his kissable lips.

It's new and unfamiliar, and I don't know how to feel about it.

She barks out a laugh, holding her hands up. "Easy, tiger. I'm not going to kiss your man. I'm just saying he has nice lips."

I give myself a mental shake. I've never felt possessive over anyone before, not even Cooper.

Over the years, he's had plenty of girls he's brought home. Hell, I once watched him basically dry-hump a chick at a bar.

But that was before he kissed me and everything changed.

"He's not my man," I argue. "We're just friends."

Another glance exchanged.

River lifts a brow, hiding a grin behind her to-go coffee cup. "Whatever you say, babe. Whatever you say. Now, let's get back to the event next month."

We finish up the business talk and head to our respective duties in the shop, Maya to the inventory in the storeroom and River to the back office. I make sure the storefront is in tiptop shape, flip the open sign on, and take my spot behind the register.

When there's a slow stretch in the afternoon, I check my phone.

Cooper: Momma B called. She's putting together a care package this weekend. You want anything special?

Me: Oh! Tell her I want some of those double chocolate brownies she makes. It's been way too long since I've had some and I'm craving chocolate.

Cooper: What'd I tell you about talking about your period with me? That's a hard line in our friendship.

Me: OMG. I bleed from my vagina. Get over it.

Me: Also, I'm not even on my period, so you're the one who brought it up, not me.

Cooper: Whatever.

Cooper: Anything else you want?

Cooper: Also, why didn't she just text you? Why do I always have to be the middleman?

Me: Why do you say that like you're some drug dealer?

Cooper: Because her baked goods are like drugs. Proof: Neither of us are even sugar fiends and we love them.

Me: I swear she puts cocaine in her brownies…

Cooper: That's powdered sugar. We've been over this.

Cooper: Don't roll your eyes at me, Caroline.

Me: Don't boss me around, Cooper.

Cooper: You love it when I boss you around.

Me: I also love it when you stop talking.

Cooper: Sorry. Can't hear you.

Me: We're texting. You don't need to hear me.

Cooper: Damn this bad connection.

What a nerd.

I roll my eyes at him. He always uses the "bad connection" excuse to get off the phone.

"What has you smiling? Oh, is it one of those alien comics where they talk all proper and it's so awkward it's hilarious?"

"Huh?" I glance up from my phone. "No. It was Cooper."

River smiles knowingly, and I have the urge to roll my eyes at her too, because she's reading way too much into it when I'm sitting here thinking how nice it is to text like things are normal between us.

"Anyway," she says, resting her arms against the counter. "I wanted to talk to you about something…"

I hold back my sigh because I have a feeling I know what's coming next.

I steeple my hands together, resting my chin on them. "Shoot."

"So, you know how we have the Harristown Jubilee in a month…"

She pauses, probably waiting for me to interrupt her.

I don't.

"I was thinking…it's a huge community thing, and people *love* supporting each other here. They want to buy local and buy handmade. So…"

"River," I say when she pauses again. "We both know where this is going. Just get to the point already."

"Right." She flashes a quick smile. "Well, since we both know, I want you to put your pieces up. Like, I want you to showcase them at the festival. Front and center. I want it to be what everyone sees first when they come to our truck."

I push my shoulders back, sitting up straight, surprised.

I knew she was going to ask me to put a few pieces in the lineup, but this? This is big.

We're both well aware that this event is *the* event of the year. It's what paid for the rest of the mobile truck we saved all year for. It's what pays for our Christmas bonuses.

Asking me to put my stuff out there is big. Asking me to put it front and center…*wow.*

If I fail, we fail, and that's an important thing to shoulder.

I'm sure you're talented, Caroline, but your silly hobby isn't going to pay your bills. You need a real career.

My dad's words float through my mind like they always do when I get excited about designing.

I like to think I'm a decent designer, but front-window-worthy? There's no way.

Sensing my hesitation, River reaches across the counter, covering my hands with hers.

"Look, I know it's a big ask, but you're a fantastic designer, Caroline. Don't think I don't pay attention to what you stroll in here wearing." She nods toward the top I have on, which used to be a blanket and is now a fringe sweater. "You have an eye for this. You're trendy while still being unique, and I think your pieces will really make us stand out this year. This place is a hodgepodge of local talent, and I want you to be a part of it."

She squeezes my hands.

"Just think it over, okay? Even if you come to me at the last minute and decide you want in, I'll make it happen. If you don't want to, that's fine too. I just had to put this out there since you're on this kick of trying new things, like macking on your best friend."

I smile when she winks.

"Thank you," I tell her. "I'm really not sure I'm ready, but I promise to think it over."

Her eyes spark with hope as she pushes off the counter. "It's not a yes, but it's not a definite no either, so I'll take it." She brushes her hands together. "My work here is done, then. I'm going to get back to poring over the inventory. I have to be out of here on time tonight or Dean said he's going to storm the store and carry me out. *Again.*"

River has a bad habit of spending too much time at work, and though she's gotten better about it since she started dating Dean, she still gets in these *I need to do all the things and need to do them now* modes. He's always there to support her...and drag her back to reality, sometimes literally.

"I saw the look on your face when he hauled you over his shoulder. You totally liked it."

"I *do* like it when he smacks my ass." She bounces her brows up and down, grinning, and her eyes get that now familiar lovestruck haze in them as she starts to think about Dean.

With a giggle, probably because she's thinking dirty thoughts, she practically skips to her office.

I let her offer simmer the rest of the afternoon.

I have pieces ready. Not a lot and they're mostly just in my size, but the design is there and that's always the hardest part. The festival is a month away. It'd take some work to make new pieces in varied sizes, but it's doable. Not like I have a social life anyway.

River was right—I have been trying new things lately.

Like dating apps. Going out to a bar.

Kissing Cooper.

Maybe I'm finally ready to put my fears aside and try this too.

"YOU'RE HOME EARLY."

Cooper sets the coffee pot back under the basket and rests his back against the counter, bringing the mug to his lips. I don't know how he can drink coffee all day long like that and still sleep a full eight hours. He must be some sort of magician. It's the only explanation I have.

I pull my crossbody purse off and hang it on the hooks we have near the door. "Yeah, River was dead set on getting out on time tonight. She was scared Dean would barge into the store and make a scene."

I took the long way, needing to think, and I still walked in the door earlier than I usually do.

"Like that's a real threat. She loves it when he does that."

I laugh. "That's what I said."

"Man, those two are ridiculous. I really didn't think they'd ever get their shit together."

"Still can't believe I lost fifty bucks in the building bet."

"I can. I told you they were fucking."

"Don't say it like that—so crassly."

"People fuck, Caroline. Well, except for you." I flip him off, and he laughs. "Speaking of, guess that gives you more time to prep for your date now that you're home early." He lifts the cup to his mouth and takes a sip, not bothering to blow on the hot liquid like the psychopath he is. "You nervous?"

I shake my head, slipping my jacket off my shoulders and putting it over my purse. "No."

"Really? Not even a little bit? It's been a while since you've been on a date."

"I'm not going."

I'm not?

I pause for a brief second, surprised by my own words.

I'm not going. I'm canceling.

Somewhere between the store and home, I decided going out with Jason isn't a smart idea. What if things are awful and it ruins my favorite bookstore? Can't go risking my book obsession.

Right. Just keep telling yourself that's the reason you're not going.

"You're not?" He pushes off the counter to his full height, going into protective mode. "What happened?"

I shrug, toeing off my flats. "Nothing happened."

"Care..." he starts, tilting his head, his brow going up in that *Don't bullshit me* way of his.

I cross the apartment to the kitchen, opening the fridge and pulling out a can of flavored water. I pop the top and take a long drink before wiping the back of my hand across my mouth.

"Really, Coop." I shrug, pushing myself up onto the counter, my favorite spot to sit. "Nothing happened."

"Then why aren't you going?" he asks, turning around to face me.

He takes another drink from his coffee, the muscles in his arms that are threatening to pop out of his plain gray t-shirt flexing with the movement.

We've spent many moments in this exact same position. Me sitting in my spot, legs bouncing off the cabinets. Him leaning against the counter opposite, one bare foot crossed over the other. Him sipping on his coffee, me drinking flavored water.

It's comfortable. *We're* comfortable.

Easy. Simple.

We make sense together.

How am I just now seeing this?

"Did he cancel on you? I knew something was off about that guy."

"No. I'm the one canceling."

"What? Why?" He sighs. "Come on. You can't keep being too shy to get out there and date. You'll never get laid if you don't try."

116

"I've been thinking about that. Maybe I jumped the gun on the whole thing."

"Is there even a gun for you to jump? You haven't been out with anyone in nearly a year."

I lift a brow. "You keeping track of my sex life now?"

"What? No." He scoffs. "I don't care if you get laid or not."

"Really? You're pushing this a little hard, don't you think?"

His hands tighten around his mug, and his jaw jumps with how hard his teeth are clenched together.

I wonder if he's doing the same thing I am...trying to force one thing to forget about another.

"I'm not. Just trying to be a good *friend* is all."

Another tic in his jaw.

"Right," I say. "*Friend.*"

I take another pull from my drink, and he swallows down the rest of his.

He sets his coffee mug down on the counter harder than necessary.

"I'm going to take a shower."

Chapter 9

COOPER

FRIEND.

Fuck, I'm really starting to hate that word.

Being a good friend to your best friend is hard to do when everything inside you wants to haul her into your lap and kiss her until neither of you can breathe.

I stopped the other night because Caroline asked, not because I wanted to.

I wanted to kiss her again. To taste her.

To see if what happened last Friday was a fluke or not.

How can something that felt so fucking good be a fluke?

Despite what happened, things have been good between us. Normal. Back to the same routine as before.

At least that's what it looks like to anyone else.

We're putting more distance between us than there has been, both physically and emotionally. We're smiling, but the expression never reaches our eyes. We're talking, but we're not really saying anything.

Things have changed. *We've* changed.

That once easy dynamic isn't so easy, and it's all fallen apart in a matter of days.

Part of me wants to take it all back: the incident in the hall, the kiss, and everything after. I want to go back to what we had before.

But I want to see what we could have even more, and I have no idea how to fucking tell her that when it's clear she doesn't want the same thing.

I close myself into the bathroom and crank the water all the way up, letting the steam fill the room as I strip off my basketball shorts and tee.

I step into the tub, pull the curtain closed, and sigh when the water hits my back.

I've been so knotted up over things with Caroline that I'm *literally* knotting up. Normally I'd ask her to use the foam roller on my back and work out the kinks, but I don't think having her straddle me is the best idea right now.

Unless she's straddling my lap...

My cock stirs to life, and I try to ignore the throbbing that seems to be a constant as of late.

Instead, I reach for the shampoo and pour a good amount on my hands, then scrub at my hair.

I wonder how good Caroline's fingers would feel doing this, if they'd feel as good as they did when they were in my hair last time...

"Fuck!" I shout, smacking the wall in frustration.

"Cooper?"

I freeze when I realize she's right outside the door.

I just wanted a few minutes alone not thinking about her.

"You okay in there?" she calls.

"Fine!" I shout back, maybe a little too aggressively.

I don't hear her say anything else, shoving myself back under the water, drowning out her voice, and all my thoughts of her.

When the fuck did she get so stuck in my head?

When did she become all I can think about?

When did I start having *feelings* for my best friend?

I realized days ago it goes beyond anything sexual when I missed her.

Not her touch or her lips.

Her.

The annoying way she always slaps her legs when she finds something truly funny. The references to those ridiculous TV shows she loves. How she always drinks all the good flavored water and leaves me with the gross ones. Fuck, I even miss her always rolling her eyes at me.

I miss those trivial things about her that she's holding back on now.

She's scared. Shy. Walking the straight and narrow. Playing it safe.

It's like she's reverted to the same Caroline she was the summer I met her.

Quiet and cautious. Unsure about me.

And I fucking hate it.

I hate that we did this to ourselves.

But I hate even more how much I want to do it again.

The water starts to run cold, and I realize I haven't even washed my body yet.

I squirt some bodywash onto the loofa and quickly wash up, rinsing off before the water really starts to freeze.

I turn it off, step out of the tub, and begin to dry off.

I realize my mistake then.

I forgot to grab new clothes.

"Fucking hell." I sigh. "Not again."

I push my clothes into the corner, not wanting to carry my dirty laundry through the house, and wrap my towel *extra* tight around my lower body.

"Here goes nothing," I mutter, pulling the door open.

The steam billows out around me, and I look down the hall toward the living room, listening for the pad of her feet.

Nothing.

I crane my neck the other direction...and my eyes collide right with Caroline's.

Her bedroom door is open, and she's sitting at her sewing desk.

Staring right at me.

Her eyes flit down my body, and her stare somehow feels even hotter than it did before.

Catching herself before her eyes travel too far, she snaps her attention back to my face.

Need.

It's right there in her gaze.

She wants me just as badly as I want her.

She swallows once, twice.

And then slowly drops her head to the work in front of her.

Don't say anything, Cooper. Don't say anything at all. Go to your room.

"You could at least buy me dinner next time."

She lifts her head, brows crushed together. "Huh?"

"If you're going to eye-fuck me, the least you could do is buy me dinner first."

Her face twists in anger, then she pushes up from her chair, stomping to her bedroom door.

"You're a real dick, Cooper Bennett."

And she slams it closed.

Good. I'd rather her be mad at me than walking on eggshells.

My hand is on my door when hers flies open again.

"Screw you, Cooper!" she hollers, charging down the hall toward me, not stopping until she's a foot away. "You know, this is all your fault. You're the one who took a shower and left his clothes in his bedroom. It wasn't my fault you didn't follow our rules."

"We have rules for showering? Since when?"

"Since always!" She throws her hands into the air. "Since we were teens and I grew boobs. We don't do nudity, and we don't do details about sex. You've stayed in your lane and I've stayed in mine. We've *always* had those unspoken rules. It's why I stopped wearing a bikini around you when we were seventeen. It's why I always wear a bra around the apartment even though I'd really rather let my boobs breathe. It's why I cover my eyes when there's a sex scene on TV. We have lines, Cooper."

"That's stupid. We're adults—we shouldn't have to tiptoe around each other."

"We do if we're going to remain friends and not let things like passing sexual desires ruin everything we've built."

"Is that what you have for me, Caroline?" I lean into her space, wanting to look into her eyes to see her answer. "Sexual desires?"

She curls her lips, darting her gaze away from mine. "I said passing."

I smile victoriously, stretching to my full height and crossing my arms over my chest. "That's not a no."

She growls, waving a hand through the air. "That's not what this is about."

"Isn't it though? Isn't it exactly what this is about? How we have these lines we're not supposed to cross, yet we did anyway?"

"*You* did." She takes a step toward me, poking her finger into my chest. "*You're* the one who walked out in nothing but a towel."

I match her step. "And you're the one who looked at me like you wanted to fuck me."

She gasps, and her eyes grow two sizes.

She takes another step closer. "You're the one who kissed me."

I match it again. "And you're the one who kissed me back."

"It was a fluke."

"Is that what you're telling yourself?"

Her nostrils flare.

And then we're kissing.

I don't know who grabbed for who, but it's happening, and I don't want to let go or think about it too much.

She grunts when her back falls against the nearest wall, but we don't break our contact. I press against her, caging her in and pushing my tongue inside her sweet mouth.

She moans the moment our tongues meet, and I drive my hips into her. The towel I'm wearing is restricting, but there's no way she doesn't feel how hard my cock is through the thin pajama shorts she changed into. I shove a knee between her legs, and she rocks against it almost at once, like she's been waiting for something to take the edge off.

I cup her jaw, tilting her head to get just the angle I want, and I devour her like I've been wanting to for days. I slide my hands into her blonde locks, letting the silky waves slip through my fingers.

She feels good. *So* fucking good. Just as good as she did before. Hell, even better.

Kissing Caroline is like a drug, and I don't think I ever want to come down from this high.

When I nibble on her bottom lip, she gasps and clutches my biceps, gliding up over my shoulders and back down my chest, fingertips tracing all the grooves of my abs. She dances her digits back up, over my neck, and buries her hands in my hair, holding me to her.

Or pushing me away.

She wrenches her mouth from mine, her hands moving to my chest, holding me at a distance as she gasps for air.

Her touch burns into me, marking me for life, I'm sure of it.

"What…" she starts, gulping in another breath. "What are we doing here, Cooper?"

"Kissing."

A grin pulls at the corner of her lips, and she lets her hands drop away. I don't waste a second, closing the gap between us again.

I grab her chin between my finger and thumb, tilting her face up so our eyes meet.

Her baby blues are full of worry and want. Questions she doesn't want to voice.

She's looking to me for help, yet she's so scared of the answer.

She pulls her plump bottom lip between her teeth. The movement has me wanting to kiss her all over again.

And I do.

I use my thumb to pull it free, then I lean forward and suck it between my own lips, kissing away the red spot she created.

She moans, and we're lost again.

Her hands fall to my hips, holding me tightly like she's scared to let go and face reality.

I'm scared too…of not ever feeling this again.

I've kissed plenty of women, but I've never felt anything like this before.

Anything this natural.

Pure.

Raw.

I drag my mouth from hers, trailing kisses over her jaw, toward that spot just below her ear I've been wanting to kiss since we danced together.

"Coop…" she pleads quietly when my lips meet the sensitive spot.

For reprieve or more, I'm not sure.

"Just don't overthink it," I tell her.

"We *have* to overthink it. We're best friends."

I pull back, looking at her.

She looks so fucking hot, her hair a mess from my hands. Lips swollen from my kisses. Eyes full of lust from my touch.

"Then let's not be best friends anymore. Let's just be us."

Her brows crumple. "What does that mean?"

"It means let's not think about anything else. Let's just

focus on what feels good. Because this…" I place a kiss on her lips. "Us…" Another kiss. "Feels good."

I drop my forehead to hers and let my lips linger against her mouth, not really kissing her, but not *not* kissing her either.

I close my eyes, breathing her in, committing the feel of her under my hands to memory just in case this is the last time I experience it.

"Tell me I'm not the only one who thinks that."

My lips brush against hers with each word, and I feel it when she lets out a soft sigh.

"You're not," she admits.

"Why do I hear a but in your voice?"

"Because what if we can't come back from this?"

"We can't. We won't."

"Is that what you want?"

"Is that what *you* want?"

Another sigh. "I don't know what I want, Cooper."

This is it. This is when she pulls away again.

"But I do know I don't want to stop kissing you."

So I don't.

I don't stop kissing her.

Not when I wrap my arm around her waist and peel her from the wall. I don't stop when I walk us back to my bedroom. And I don't dare break our kiss when I lead her to my bed, guiding her onto the mattress and fitting myself between her legs.

"Cooper," she says between kisses.

"Hmm?"

"You're wet."

"I think you meant to say *I'm wet.*"

She laughs, pulling at my hair.

I peer down at her, trying not to look disappointed she's broken our kiss yet again.

"No. *You're* wet—you're still in your towel."

Oh. Duh.

I grin. "Guess we'll just have to get rid of it, then."

Her eyes widen, and I can see the fear.

"Hey, if you don't want to do anything other than kiss, that's fine. If you want to ride my cock until the sun comes up, that's cool too."

Her face flushes, and I wonder if she's thinking about riding me.

Because I sure as fuck am thinking about it.

My cock grows impossibly hard at the thought of her on top of me, her big tits bouncing as she rides me and I play with her clit.

Fuck, she looks so beautiful beneath me. Like she was meant to be in my bed. I want nothing more than to strip us both naked and make us both feel good.

But I'll follow her lead on this one.

"It sounds so weird to hear you say that to me of all people."

"Bad weird?"

She shakes her head. "No...good. But I'm also still trying to get used to the fact that my best friend makes my girly parts go berserk."

"Is that what I make happen?" I say, leaning down, running my lips up her neck, back to that spot just below her ear that made her moan.

"Y-Yes."

"Tell me, Caroline," I whisper into her ear, "have you been thinking about me naked?"

I drive my hips into her, and she whimpers when my dick brushes against her sex.

"Maybe a few times."

"Just a few?" I ask, doing it again.

She gulps. "Okay, maybe more than a few times."

"Did you touch yourself thinking about me?"

She exhales a shaky breath. "N-No. I wanted to, but I didn't. It felt like crossing a line."

I nip at the sensitive spot I haven't stopped teasing with my mouth. "Does this feel like crossing a line?"

"So much," she says.

Another nip. Another moan.

"Cooper?"

"Yeah?"

"Take the towel off."

Chapter 10

CAROLINE

"TAKE THE TOWEL OFF."

Cooper lifts his head and peers down at me. "Are you sure?"

I nod.

His captivating pale eyes are searching mine for any hint of uncertainty.

There is none.

I'm absolutely certain I want Cooper to take the towel off.

I need to see him. To feel him.

To *touch* him.

Right now, I want him, and I'm tired of running from it.

We'll figure everything else out tomorrow.

Tonight, I want this.

"Say it," he urges. "I need to hear you say it."

"I'm sure."

Without hesitation, he pushes himself off the bed. I hate losing the warmth of him, but I'm eager to see what comes next.

He holds his hand out to me.

"What?" I ask, looking down at it.

"If I'm getting naked, you are too. Fair is fair."

I can't argue with that.

I slip my hand into his, letting him pull me up to a standing position.

We're only inches apart, but now that I know what it feels like to be wrapped in his arms, it feels like miles.

He reaches out to me, running his finger over the buttons on my top, probably realizing that if he undresses me, all bets are off.

Right now, I want them off, just like I want this shirt off.

I pop the top button loose.

Cooper curses.

And I undo another.

He watches, eyes dilated with lust as I deftly unbutton the rest.

His eyes grow darker at the sight of my shirt hanging open on my shoulders, my bra visible to him for the first time.

"Jesus," he mutters, reaching out like he can't help himself, tracing a single finger over the swell of my breasts. "So much fucking lace."

Then, without warning, he pushes my top down my arms, letting it fall to the floor around us.

He doesn't stop there, fitting his hands around my waist like they were made to hold me, slipping his fingers into the waistband of my shorts.

His eyes hold mine, waiting for me to interject.

When I don't, he hooks his fingers into the fabric and pushes the material down my legs like he's undressed me a thousand times before.

I step out of the shorts, kicking them to the side.

He takes a step back, letting his eyes wander over me with his bottom lip tucked between his teeth.

This is the most exposed I've ever been to him.

I thought I'd be more scared of this part. Too nervous to stand before him like this.

I'm not.

It feels so…right.

Natural.

Like being with Cooper like this is where I was always supposed to be.

"They match?" he asks, his eyes still scanning my body, surprised to see that my bra and panties do indeed match.

I nod, so happy I wore my lacy pale pink set tonight.

"For him?" he asks, referring to my long-forgotten date.

I shake my head. "No. They always do."

"*This* is what you've been hiding from me all these years?"

It's a question, but not one he really wants an answer to.

He mutters something I can't quite make out, then slides his gaze to mine.

"You're so fucking sexy, Caroline."

Now I'm blushing.

He's complimented me before, but the way he's rasping out his words now… It's a whole different level.

He steps into me, tucking my hair behind my ear and tilting my chin up.

"I need to know you're one hundred percent okay with this. Because if I take this towel off, there's no going back."

"I'm still wearing something," I counter.

"Not for long," he promises, his eyes darker than I've ever seen them before.

I gulp.

Am I ready? Do I want this?

Yes.

"I want you, Cooper."

He closes his eyes, pressing his forehead against mine. "Fuck I love hearing you say that." I hear him swallow. "I want to take my time. I want to be gentle. But I...I don't know if I can."

"Then don't. I don't want you to hold back. I want *you*. All of you."

The words are barely out of my mouth before his lips are on mine and he's kissing me harder than he ever has before, hands crashing through my hair.

He pulls away just as fast, still holding on to me.

"Take your panties off and get on the bed."

"What?" I ask, my head all fuzzy from the kiss.

"The bed," he tells me, putting distance between us. "Take your panties off and get on the bed."

I nod and reach behind my back to unhook my bra, but he stops my efforts. "No. Later."

"But—"

"I said later."

His voice is firm. Rough.

I've never heard him like this before, but I've also never been like this with him before.

I like it. *A lot.*

I nod again, licking my lips, and follow his instructions. I push my panties down my legs, stepping out of them and kicking them toward my shorts.

I turn, dropping a knee onto the bed. Cooper strikes my

ass with an open palm...*hard.* I gasp and a rush of pleasure shoots through parts of me I didn't expect.

"You good?" he asks, and I nod.

He does it again.

It hurts, but in a good kind of way.

Jesus. No wonder River likes it when Dean smacks her ass.

"Keep going," he says, massaging where he struck me, then patting me encouragingly. "Against the headboard."

I do as he says, turning to face him.

I don't know what to do with my hands. Don't know how to sit.

It feels so strange having him stand at the end of the bed watching me, yet so hot having his devoted attention.

"Spread your legs."

I gulp, and my breathing picks up at the request.

He dips his head toward me. "Do it, Caroline."

Has he always said my name like that? With that rasp? With that authority like he owns me and he knows it?

Slowly, I spread my legs.

And Cooper lets out another string of curses, dropping his hand to his hard cock for the first time, squeezing it through the towel he's still wearing.

"Perfect," he murmurs. "Absolutely fucking perfect."

My entire body is on fire—from my blushing so hard due to being so exposed, and from the pure need burning through me due to how incredibly turned on I am under his hungry gaze.

"Wider."

I oblige.

I guarantee if I were to move right now, there'd be a wet spot soaking through his sheets.

"Touch yourself."

This time I don't even try to argue or hesitate.

I want it as bad as he does.

I slip my hand between my legs, sliding two fingers between my folds, drawing small circles over my swollen clit.

"Son of a..."

He drops the towel.

I'm not a saint—I've seen Cooper around the house in sweatpants. A girl pays attention to things like that, especially when the outline of his dick is always so evident.

But I wasn't expecting him to be *this* big.

He fists his cock, pumping it once. Twice.

He's breathtaking.

Thighs parted, washboard abs on full display. Those strong shoulders of his moving as he strokes himself.

"Finger yourself."

I pull my eyes up.

"Show me you want me to fuck you, Caroline."

Every time he says my name, it makes something inside my chest flutter.

It's like he wants to remind me that he knows it's me sitting across from him.

Like he wants to remind himself.

This is real. This is happening.

I slide a finger inside my pussy, pushing it in and out.

He chuckles darkly.

"Oh, baby, you're going to need more than that to be ready for me."

A moan bubbles out of me at the thought of Cooper's cock

stroking inside of me, and I add another finger, my pussy gripping it tight.

I pump my fingers slowly as he watches, slowly stroking himself in time with my movements, his bottom lip trapped tightly between his teeth.

"More."

I add a third finger.

"Harder," he says, one knee going to the edge of the bed like he can't help but come closer to me. "I'm going to take you a lot harder than that."

Take you.

I nearly combust at his words, heeding his request not just because he asked but because I need it now too.

"Fuck," he mutters. "Come here."

I crawl to where he stands, feeling awkward on my hands and knees until I see him stroke his length faster, watching me intently.

When I'm close, he reaches out, pulling me up to my knees, his mouth capturing mine in a rough kiss.

He moves lower, nipping down my chin and my neck, over the swell of my breasts. I toss my head back in pleasure when he closes his mouth around my nipple over my bra, loving the way the lace brushes against me as his tongue swirls over the hardened bud.

His teeth clamp around my nipple, biting me just hard enough for it to teeter on the edge of pain and pleasure.

I gasp, and he does it again.

I don't even realize he's unhooked my bra until I feel the cool air hit my tits. A shiver runs through me, goose bumps rising across my skin.

In the two seconds he's gone, I miss his mouth.

Then he's back, covering one with his lips again and palming the other.

He teases me, moving between each breast, giving them equal amounts of attention until I'm practically squirming under his assault.

"Cooper…" I gasp when he nips at me again.

He laughs, and I feel the vibrations everywhere.

I want more. I *need* more.

I reach for his cock and he shifts his hips back.

I groan.

Another laugh.

He pulls his mouth from my chest, my nipples hard and swollen from his kisses, trailing back up to my ear, sucking and licking at me on the ascent. I love how his stubble feels against my skin, rough but so damn good.

"Caroline," he whispers against me. "I want to feel my cock in your mouth."

I pant at his words, my thighs shaking with need.

"Will you let me fuck your mouth?"

"*Yes.*"

The voice that leaves my lips sounds nothing like mine.

It's raspy. Broken. *Pleading.*

He seals his mouth over mine in a hard kiss, then peels me off him.

"If you want me to stop, tell me."

I nod, but I already know there will be nothing to tell.

I kiss down his chest, over his abs, and don't stop until his hard cock brushes against my chin.

With gentle fingers, he gathers my hair, wrapping it tightly around his fist.

"Look at me," he instructs.

I drag my eyes to his.

"Open."

I do.

"Flatten your tongue."

I listen.

"Good girl," he says, and he guides his cock into my waiting mouth.

He strokes himself against me. His thick, smooth shaft gliding over my tongue, pushing deeper with each pass, warming me up for his length.

I can taste the pre-cum leaking from his head, and I'm already eager for more.

"You ready?" he asks.

I nod.

He pushes into me with no restraint, fucking my mouth as he promised. He tightens his grip on my hair, watching as his cock slips past my lips over and over again. He goes deeper each time until he's seated in the back of my throat, pausing for just a moment before he starts again.

He's rough. Unapologetic.

And I love every second of it.

I slip my hand back between my legs, inserting two fingers into my pussy because I can't *not* touch myself right now.

"Is that what you want?" he asks. "You want my cock inside of you?"

I groan around him, pumping faster.

Without warning, he pulls free and hauls me back to my knees.

"Up the bed. On your back. Legs spread."

He kisses me hard, then lets me go, stroking his cock that's now glistening with my saliva.

I follow his orders, watching as he moves through the room, reaching into the top drawer of his bedside table and grabbing a condom.

He covers himself, then covers me with his body.

"Good?" he asks as he fits himself between my thighs, wrapping one of my thighs around him.

I answer with a kiss.

He slips his tongue into my mouth as he slips into me.

Even with the preparation, the sting of him stretching me still hurts. He swallows my groans, rocking in and out of me slowly, letting me get used to him.

He's holding back and I know it.

I don't want him to hold back.

I want him. I want *all* of him.

"Cooper…" I pant between kisses. "Let go."

"Oh, thank fuck," he says, pulling his mouth away.

His hands find my wrists and he holds my arms above my head as he surges into me, letting go of everything he was holding back.

"*Oh god,*" I cry out as he drives into me until he's all the way in.

It's like he was made to fit inside of me.

I feel every stroke, every ridge of him.

I'm on a whole new level of high as he pumps in and out of me. I don't think I can ever get over this feeling. Nothing will ever be the same again, and I'm not sure I want it to.

He lets go of one of my wrists and moves my hand between us.

"Touch yourself. Get there with me."

I do, stroking my clit to match his movements as he puts both hands on his headboard and plunges into me faster. Harder. Beads of sweat drip down his chest and roll over his abs.

He looks so beautiful, so powerful driving into me. Seeing Cooper in such a raw state is exhilarating, and I don't think anything will ever look as good as he does right now.

"I'm close," I tell him, my eyes beginning to flutter closed as my orgasm edges closer.

"Open," he barks. "I want to see you fall apart."

A few more strokes, and I do.

My pussy clenches around him, and with another few pumps, he falls right behind me.

His strokes slow, his breaths coming in short pants along with mine.

My heart is beating so loud that if it weren't for our gasps for air filling the room, I'm certain he would hear it.

"Shit," he mutters, closing his eyes and resting his forehead on the headboard. "We are so fucked."

And he's right.

WE ARE SO FUCKED.

It's my first thought when I peel my eyes open, looking around the familiar room.

Cooper's room.

The last thing I remember is Cooper collapsing next to me, curling his arm around my waist, and pulling me tightly against him. His lips ghosted over the back of my neck over and over, the light touches soothing and everything I didn't realize I needed in the moment.

I waited for the panic to set in. I guess I fell asleep waiting. Judging from the now dark sky, at least an hour has passed, if not more.

What time is it?

"It's almost eight." His hoarse voice slices through the quiet room like a thunderous boom. "You fell asleep."

"Did you?" I ask.

"A little."

We fall quiet again, the only sound the fans on his computer.

I'm not sure how long we stay like that, me with my head on his chest, lying in the quiet, but it's long enough for his breathing to even out, and I wonder if he's fallen asleep.

I slept with my best friend.

And it was easily the best sex I've ever had.

Like so good I already know I'm one hundred percent ruined for life. I don't think anyone else could possibly make me feel that good again.

The panic that was missing before starts to creep in.

What did I do? What did we do?

"Stop."

His voice is commanding, but nothing near what it was when he was inside of me.

I didn't realize Cooper had that side to him. Sure, he's bossy as hell on a good day, but I never knew it carried over into the bedroom.

I never thought I'd like it so much either.

"Stop what?" I ask.

Instead of answering, he hauls me on top of him, moving me around with ease until I'm straddling him.

I don't miss his hard cock rubbing against my ass.

"Stop thinking about it."

"Your cock on my ass or the fact that I had the best sex of my life and it was with my best friend?"

He lifts a brow, and I have the urge to reach up and push it back down.

"Best sex of your life, huh?"

A blush steals up my cheeks.

His chest rumbles with laughter. "Little late to get all shy now, isn't it?"

"Shut up," I grumble, trying to scramble off him, but it's no use. His big hands hold me just where I am, not letting me run.

He swats my ass when I struggle against him, and a moan slips free.

"Stop squirming." He grips my hips tighter, that sting of pain and pleasure I'm learning to love biting at me again.

"Man, you're bossy," I complain.

"You like it."

I lift a shoulder. "It's okay."

He shifts his hips, his hard length pressing harder between my ass cheeks. "Do I need to remind you how much you like it?"

"N-No."

"That's what I thought." He reaches up, brushing a lock of hair behind my ear. "How do you feel?"

"Physically?" He nods. "Like Jell-O."

He chuckles, dancing his fingers down my chest and to my right breast, which is *definitely* bruised from his love bites. He gently runs his fingertip across it, and my nipple hardens under his touch.

"I wasn't too rough?"

I shake my head. "No. But it was…surprising how rough you were."

"Good or bad surprising?"

"Good," I whisper. "Very good."

He grins wolfishly as he continues to swirl his finger around my nipple, watching it move over the sensitive bud.

Longing stirs between my legs, and it's crazy how such a simple touch can make my body feel like it's on fire, even after all we've already done tonight.

I should be tired. I *am* tired.

But I want him again even more.

His thick brows furrow together. "And emotionally?" He meets my eyes, pausing his gentle strokes. "How are you feeling emotionally, Caroline?"

There it is again, that tone when he says my name.

Confident. Like he knows he has me all wrapped up inside.

"I'm…okay. A little confused and scared. But mostly okay."

"Scared?" I nod. "Of what?"

"This." I swallow thickly. "Of how good it feels."

"It does feel good, doesn't it?"

"I don't just mean physically," I tell him. "It's…other ways."

"I knew exactly what you meant."

I drop my head, shaking it. I look at my hands pressed on his chest, curling my fingers into the hair that's smattered across it. It feels so…normal.

"This is all so strange, Cooper," I admit.

"I know."

"I mean, look at us. I'm straddling you—naked, I might add—while your cock is rubbing against my ass. I'm getting wetter by the second just thinking of what transpired between us and how much I want to do it again."

Heat blazes in his eyes, and a grin pulls at his lips.

"Well, I wasn't going to say anything about the wet part..."

I swat at his chest. "Stop it! This is *embarrassing*."

He laughs. "It's not embarrassing for me. You're over here lamenting on about my massive cock and all the ways I make you horny. Baby, this is heaven."

"I never said a single word about your massive cock."

"So you agree? You think it's massive?"

Another blush. "Cooper..."

He shakes with laughter, gripping my hips, knowing me well enough to know I'll try to run again if he doesn't hold me still.

Except with where he has me trapped, I feel his cock rubbing against my ass, and I don't think I'll ever want to run from that.

"I'm teasing. Sort of."

"How are you feeling?" I ask him.

"Physically?" I nod. "Like Jell-O," he echoes.

I grin. "And emotionally?"

He sighs. "The same as you, I think. This is completely unfamiliar territory and it's a little strange, but it also feels..."

"Natural?"

"I was going to say wet."

I smack at him again, and he chuckles, grabbing my wrists.

"Stop hitting me."

"Stop teasing me."

"I wouldn't be *me* if I didn't tease." He sets my hands back on his chest. "And I am, Caroline. I'm still me, okay? And you're still you. I don't want to forget that. We have history and I don't want to just pretend we don't, but I also don't want that history to get in the way of whatever's happening here."

"You mean you want me to forget about that time you tried to jump the fence to the quarry, fell, and farted so loud it echoed and the guards caught us?"

"God yes. Don't ever think about that again."

"I don't know…it's kind of burned into my brain forever."

"Caroline…"

I giggle when he dances his hands up my sides, tickling me. "I'm kidding, I'm kidding! It's all forgotten."

"Good."

He relents his torture, then pulls me down, capturing my mouth with a slow, languid kiss.

The wetness between my legs grows at every stroke of his tongue against mine. I'm ready for more, and I'm just about to ask for it when he tugs his mouth away.

He snickers at the growl that bubbles out of me.

"Now, do me another favor, would you?"

"Anything," I promise.

"Ride my cock."

And I do.

Chapter 11

COOPER

I'VE BEEN WATCHING Caroline sleep for the last hour like a complete fucking creep.

I just can't stop thinking if I blink too hard, she's going to disappear. Or I'll wake up and this will have just been a really, *really* fucking good dream.

I can't believe this is happening.

She had it right—we do feel natural together. Right in all the ways you can imagine.

There wasn't a moment that I didn't feel comfortable with her, that I was embarrassed by what we were doing. It was easy. Effortless. Like it was what we were made for.

And fuck do I want to do it again.

She stirs beside me, arms rising above her head as she stretches. She groans and rubs at her eyes.

"I can feel you staring." A smile tugs at her lips. "It woke me up, you creep."

"So?" I don't bother feeling guilty for waking her up. Waking her up means I can have my way with her again.

She turns her head my way, peeling her bright blue eyes open. "What time is it?"

"Just before six."

"Oh god." She covers her face with her hands. "It's way too early to be so creepy." She yawns, rubbing at her eyes. "What are you doing up so early anyway?"

"I couldn't sleep."

"How?" She grabs the blanket, pulling it up over her chest as she sits up next to me. "Aren't you tired?"

"You mean from all the sex you kept begging me for? Yes." She rolls her eyes. "It's way too early for you to be rolling your eyes."

"You asked for it." She combs her fingers through her hair. "Seriously, why are you awake? You don't have to start work for another three hours."

"Couldn't sleep."

She sends me a knowing glance. "Couldn't, or didn't want to?"

"That obvious?"

"No. I guess I just understand. This all feels…"

"Like a wet dream?"

She laughs. "Or just a dream."

"No, it's definitely wet. I'm sitting in it."

"Ew." She wrinkles her nose. "That's definitely your fault, not mine."

"I'm sorry, am I the one who leaks from their orifices?"

"First of all, don't say *orifices* when you have a girl naked in your bed. Second, you do come, right?"

I raise a brow, smirking. "I think you know the answer to that as well as I do."

She blushes, likely thinking of the same thing I am—her

sucking me off until I spilled down her throat after we got out of the shower.

"Right. Then we're both aware you do. So that means *you* can leak too."

I shrug. "Semantics."

She starts to roll her eyes again but thinks better of it.

She turns her head, peering around the room she's been in thousands of times before but never in this capacity. I'd be doing the same thing in her position.

"Can I ask you something?" she says quietly.

"Hmm?"

"This...us...what made you want it?"

"You mean besides watching you parade around the apartment for seven years in those ratty-ass pajamas and mud masks once a week?"

She huffs, and I laugh.

"Honestly, I don't know," I say, lifting a shoulder. "It just sort of snuck up on me. *You* snuck up on me."

"Was it the hallway incident?"

"That was a big part of it, yes. I wasn't expecting your reaction to seeing me like that. And I wasn't expecting how much I liked you seeing me like that."

She nods. "That's what started it for me too. Have you ever..." I don't have to look at her to know she's blushing. "You know...thought about me like that before? Before last week, I mean."

"Do you want the truth?"

"From you? Always."

"Yes," I tell her. "I've thought about it, but not too hard and not intentionally. Not one of those, *Man, today I'm going to sit around and masturbate to my best friend because I'm secretly in love with her* things. It was more of *My best friend is hot and I'm a horny teen* sort of deals. It never went beyond that though."

"And now?" She tucks a strand of hair behind her ear. "What do you think now?"

"Well, I still think you're pretty damn hot."

"Pretty damn hot?"

"Yeah. I definitely wasn't aware of that mole on your ass."

"Cooper!" I hold my arm up against the onslaught of the pillow she's throwing my way. "I do not have a mole on my ass!"

"Fine, fine," I say, snatching the pillow from her and chucking it across the room. "Mole or no mole, you're hot. Beautiful. *Sexy.*"

"That's much better." She crosses her arms over her chest, grinning victoriously. "But that's not what I meant."

"I know." I sigh, scrubbing a hand through my hair. "Is that what you want? A relationship?"

She takes a moment to answer, brows pinched together in concentration.

It feels like forever passes before she nods.

"Yeah, I think that's what I want. I'm not good at casual sex."

"You've never *tried* casual sex." She huffs, and I laugh. "But I know what you mean," I say. "You're definitely the relationship type, and I get that. It's just how you're wired."

"What about you?" she asks. "Have you thought about it? Us in a relationship?"

I nod. "I have."

She tugs her lip between her teeth, chewing on it. "Yeah?"

"Yeah, and I don't think it's a crazy idea. Actually, I think it makes sense. *A lot* of sense."

"In what ways?"

"All of them."

I turn toward her, reaching out and plucking her lip free. I run my thumb over the swollen flesh. She peers up at me, those big blue eyes swimming with worry, curiosity, and caution.

"When we didn't talk after Friday night, it fucking sucked. I hated it. Hated not having you here, not seeing you laugh. Hell, I'd have rather had you slap me and call me an ass for kissing you than ignoring me. It was agony, especially because I thought for sure I'd fucked things up on a whole new level. I was terrified I'd lost you for good."

She opens her mouth to speak, and I shake my head, stopping her.

"But it made me think, made me realize small things that have always bothered me and I couldn't place my finger on why. Like all those times in the past when we fought. When we ignored each other over ridiculous things like when you definitely stole my signed Kobe Bryant jersey, spilled Kool-Aid all over it, and then returned it stained, swearing up and down it wasn't you." She tucks her lips together, holding back her laugh. "We didn't talk for a week after that. I was *so* mad at you then. But I realize now it wasn't just me being upset with you over the jersey. I was mad because you weren't there…because I missed you. I just didn't know how to articulate that then."

I cup her face and pull her closer.

I press a kiss to her forehead, then lean back, peering into her eyes.

"If you want to know if I see a relationship with you now, yes. Because my life isn't the same without you in it, Caroline."

She wraps her hand around my wrist, leaning into my touch and squeezing her eyes shut tight. "This scares me so much."

"Me too."

"What if we suck together?"

"Well, you *do* suck."

"Coop..." she groans.

I laugh. "I'm sure we'll suck. All couples suck every now and then. But wouldn't it suck more if we didn't even try?"

"Are you serious about this? Because you don't do relationships. *I'm* the one who dates. You're the one who humps and dumps."

"You're right," I say, dropping my hand from her face. "You should leave. I mean, I've humped, now it's time to..."

She glares at me, and I laugh, pulling her back to me.

"I'm being serious, Cooper. Relationships are hard. I don't want to do this with you if it's not what you want."

"It is what I want."

"How do you know?" she counters. "You've never wanted a relationship before."

She's right. I haven't ever really wanted a relationship in the past—but that's because nobody ever seemed worthy of giving it a shot with.

"It's you. You're different."

It's not a line. It's the truth. She's different. She's Caroline.

"And because it feels good. *Natural.*"

She exhales slowly, softly. "You know if we do this, things are going to change between us, right?"

"I would like to point out that I ate your pussy last night when I definitely wouldn't have done that as friends, so things are already changing."

She rolls her eyes. "You're already making me regret this."

"Does that mean you want to try?"

She swallows, then slowly nods. "Yes. But I also want to be cautious. I want to be *us* still. You know those married couples who always say they married their best friend? That's what I want, to still be friends in between everything else. *Partners.*"

"Be like married couples, huh? You proposing to me, Caroline Elizabeth Reed?"

"You wish, Bennett."

"Hmm, Caroline Elizabeth Bennett has a nice ring to it."

"That's not even my middle name."

"It's not your last name either...yet."

I wink and she groans, shoving my face away.

And I know we won't suck together at all.

"ARE you really not going to turn the heat up tonight? It's getting down into the forties, Cooper. The forties!"

"Yeah, outside, and it's sixty-two in here. That's a whole twenty-plus degrees higher. Just grab an extra blanket."

She huffs. "You know, as a *boyfriend*, you should turn the heat up."

Boyfriend.

The word is still strange to hear, especially coming from Caroline's mouth directed at me, but I don't hate it.

In fact, I really kind of like it.

I've never really been a boyfriend. I've always preferred to get my rocks off and move along. Never been one to attach myself to someone. Nobody has ever seemed worth attaching to.

But I guess just like every other aspect of my life, Caroline is the exception to that rule.

Of course my true first time dipping my toes into this pool would be with my best friend.

Smart one, Cooper.

"You know, as a *girlfriend*, you shouldn't nag so much. It's really unattractive and I might have to withhold sex if you keep it up."

Her hand goes to her hip. "You're going to withhold sex? From *me*?"

"If that's what it takes."

"We'll see about that." She growls and stomps out of my bedroom.

I smile when I hear her grumbling from the living room, probably going on about what an ass I am. I know it's just a matter of minutes before she stomps back in here with the gray chinchilla blanket in hand.

It's been a few days since we decided to give whatever is happening between us a shot, and I think Caroline's plea for us to not change has been met. We're still *us*, we just kiss a lot more now.

Admittedly, that part has been an adjustment. I almost have to remind myself that it's okay to touch her. I've spent so long with her playing the *just friends* routine that I forget I don't have to hold back anymore.

And our jokes...they feel more intimate and private than before.

Now when we watch a movie, she no longer falls asleep innocently on my lap. She's too busy straddling it.

We haven't told anyone what we're doing yet. I think we're both too scared to jinx it or hear what a bad idea it is.

Momma B tried to video-chat me yesterday, then called Caroline when I didn't answer.

Neither of us could answer because my cock was buried in her throat, and we both got in trouble for not answering our phones.

The only thing I regret is not realizing sooner how good it feels to be with her like this.

Not just the sex—which is incredible—but everything else.

The looks. The simple touches. The feeling of being intimate without actually being intimate.

I didn't realize I was missing that until now.

Hell, I don't think I even realized I really wanted it until now.

I hear feet pad across the apartment, and I chuckle.

"Fine, you win—but only because I'm really starting to like your bedroom more." She barrels into the room, then climbs into my bed like it's her own, pulling my comforter *and* the gray blanket over top of her. "Did you know you can hear Mailbox Betty through my bedroom wall? Her cats are super annoying."

She fluffs the pillow—my *favorite* pillow—behind her

and sighs, letting her eyes fall closed when she leans back against it.

"Are you comfortable?" I ask, staring down at her with a raised brow.

She peels an eye open. "Very. But could you turn out the hallway light? It's shining right into my eyes when I close them."

I flip the blanket off my legs, tossing my e-reader onto the bedside table, and push off of the bed. "You're really going to take advantage of this whole boyfriend thing, aren't you?"

"Yes. But I also know you'd do it for me anyway because you love me."

We both still.

Now *that's* one part of this I didn't think about at all.

Love.

We've used that word before over the years, casually and not putting anything behind it other than platonic feelings. Because of course I love her. She's been in my life for over ten years now. How could I not love her?

But now? That word has a different meaning...a different feeling.

She clears her throat and shuffles around the bed.

I force myself to move. To not think about it too hard.

I reach into the hall and flip off the light, then make my way back to the warmth of the bed.

Shit. It actually *is* getting cold in here.

But I'm not turning up the heat and giving Caroline the satisfaction. I know she'd turn it around to how I did it just for her and not because *I* was cold too. She'd never shut up about it.

I stop at my dresser and grab an extra pair of socks.

"Are you putting more clothes on? Isn't that a little counterproductive given what's going to go on here tonight?"

"My, my, Caroline," I say, lifting the blanket and scooting back under. "Are you just using me for my body? Is that all I am to you, a plaything?"

She side-eyes me, ignoring my teasing and flipping open her sketchpad that's lying on her lap.

A folded piece of paper falls out of it, slipping down onto the blankets between us.

"What's this?" I ask, snatching up the paper. "A love note from your other boyfriend?"

"I bet he'd turn the heat up," she grumbles, trying to grab the paper from my hand.

I'm faster than her, moving it out of reach and unfolding it.

"It's nothing," she insists. "Just a silly design I was thinking of working on."

I let my eyes wander over the sketch, and I can already picture her wearing it. "This looks good." I see a note at the bottom. "Wait...does that say jubilee? Is that what this is for?"

She again tries to steal the paper and again fails.

She sighs defeatedly, picking up her sketchpad instead and flipping to a blank page. "River asked me to make some pieces for the event."

I perk up at her confession.

She's flippant about it, but I know it's a big deal. Her father really did a number on her when he refused to support her dream of designing, calling it a pipe dream and pushing her toward something more "practical."

I tried to convince her it was *her* future and not his, but

155

since she wasn't on good terms with her mom, I don't think she could bear the thought of disappointing her father.

So, she caved.

I think she's regretted it since.

"Let me guess," I say, "you told her no."

She narrows her eyes at me. "It's none of your business."

"As a boyfriend, I'm pretty sure it is."

"As a boyfriend"—she moves unexpectedly, finally managing to snatch the paper from my hands—"it's definitely not. If I want to put a few pieces up, I'll do it, and we can celebrate *if* they sell. And as a boyfriend, it's also your place to respect if I decide not to and pretend River never asked. You're not allowed to push me on this. Got it?"

I sigh, letting her win this round. "For what it's worth, I think you should do it."

"You always say I should do it when River asks."

"And I mean it every time. You're a good designer, Caroline. You should let people see your talent."

"People do see. I wear my own clothes all the time."

The dress comes to mind.

Man, the way it hugged every inch of her so perfectly. How her tits were perfectly on display. The way it slid up her legs just enough to leave me curious about what she was wearing underneath whenever she danced.

My cock twitches at the memory, and suddenly I'm disappointed I never got to peel it off her.

"Besides, you don't need to give me the speech. River already has. She's been dropping hints all week, and she only asked me a few days ago."

"Well, take whatever speech she's been giving you and

repeat it back, but do it in a deep sexy voice, so you know it's me."

"Is that what you think you have? A deep sexy voice?"

"It's what I know I have."

She shrugs. "It's okay."

I place my lips against her ear, whispering, "Just okay?"

"Yep."

"What do I have to do to convince you otherwise? Whisper dirty things into your ear?"

Her eyelids flutter shut. "It won't work."

"But I can try, can't I?"

She makes a noise when I dart my tongue out, teasing her.

"I bet you'd love for me to tell you how much I want to see you ride my cock again. How much I fantasize about watching as your sweet, *sweet* pussy stretches and takes all of me. How much I want to see you throw your head back and break apart around me as I stroke your pretty little clit."

Another soft sigh falls from her lips.

"Sh-Shut up."

I chuckle. "You don't really want that. You want to hear more, don't you? Want to hear all the dirty things I've been dying to whisper to you?"

She licks at her lips, gulping but not saying anything.

"Do you want me to tell you more dirty things?"

A gentle nod.

"The trash is overflowing and it's your turn to take it out."

I pull away from her, return to my side of the bed, pick my e-reader back up, and turn my attention back to my book with a satisfied grin.

I feel her shaking her head beside me, and I sneak a peek her way.

She's glaring at me. *Hard.*

She slips out of bed, grabbing her blanket and *my* pillow before stomping out of the room.

"Good night, Caroline!" I call out. "Sweet dreams!"

"I hate you, Cooper Bennett!"

"No you don't! And don't roll your eyes at me!"

She groans loudly, and I smirk.

An hour later, she crawls back into my bed, and all my dirty fantasies come to life.

Chapter 12

CAROLINE

"I'M STARVING."

"Hi, starving, I'm Caroline."

"Wow. I cannot believe I'm actually dating you." He squeezes my leg that's stretched out over his lap, massaging my calf. "You must be really good in the sack."

I twist my face up, peeking at him over the edge of my sketchpad, which I've been drawing in for the last hour. "Can you not say *good in the sack*? It sounds...gross."

"Fine. You must be really good at slobbing on the knob."

"Okay, that's way worse."

He laughs, moving his hands to my right foot. He nods toward the book in my hands. "What are you working on over there? Stuff for River and the festival?"

Yes. "No."

"You're lying."

"I am not."

He shakes his head. "Please. I always know when you're lying. I *know* you."

Dammit. I know he's right.

"It's nothing," I tell him, turning my attention back to my drawing. "Just a few new designs."

"For the festival?" he asks again.

"I'm...not sure yet."

He switches his ministrations to the other foot. "I think you should say yes."

"So you've said."

"And I can tell you *want* to say yes."

He's right. I *do* want to say yes. But I'm still so...scared.

Part of me wants to just push all my fears aside and run right into this opportunity. Then I watch River doing everything she can to make this event perfect and looking at me with such hope in her eyes.

And it makes me worried I'll fail and disappoint her.

Your silly hobby isn't going to pay your bills. You need a real career.

I hear my dad's voice for the millionth time.

The fear eats at me, springing right back front and center, crippling me once again.

I lay my sketchpad against my chest so he can see I'm serious. "I've told you already, Cooper—I'm not ready, okay?"

He stares at me, and I can tell he wants to say something but thinks better of it.

"Besides," I say, picking my book back up. "I don't even have actual products ready. Just sketches."

"I've seen your workspace. I know you have plenty of pieces in there."

"I don't have pieces in *multiple sizes*," I counter.

"Remember like a minute ago when I said I can tell when you're lying?" *Double dammit.* "You think I haven't seen you in there working on them? Haven't noticed that you've been putting in extra hours at night?"

"You only notice because it takes away from sexy times with you."

"Tell me about it."

He huffs, but I know he's teasing.

We spend *a lot* of time having sex. Not that I'm complaining, because it's easily the best sex I've ever had, and I don't think there's any way it could ever get better.

"Hey, Care?"

"Hmm?"

"Can you look at me?"

I peek at him over my drawings.

"I won't bug you about it again, but I think you should do it. You're a talented designer. River wouldn't ask you if she didn't believe in your product. *I* believe in your product, and you know I wouldn't lie to you. I can't." He squeezes my foot, pulling his lips up on one side. "So maybe it's time you start believing in yourself too."

I can see in his eyes he's not lying. He *does* believe in me.

A glimmer of confidence sparks back to life within my chest.

I run my tongue over my lip and blow out a heavy breath. "I'll think about it, okay? But if I say to let it go, you need to let it go. These are my issues to work out and it's not your job to fix them. Got it?"

He smashes his lips together, looking like he wants to argue. Instead, he nods once. "Okay."

"Thank you."

I return my attention to my sketchpad, and he resumes the foot rub.

I'm happy he believes in me, but that's what best friends do. It's the equivalent of your parent hanging your crappy finger painting on the fridge. It doesn't carry the same weight.

"You hungry?" he asks a few minutes later.

"Not really. There's ramen in the kitchen. Make some of that."

"Excuse me," he says, switching feet again. "I'm a sophisticated man. I'm not eating *ramen* for dinner."

"You're the one who bought the ramen."

"Yeah, for you."

"I don't even eat it!"

"Oh. Right. I guess that is mine, then." He curls his lip in disgust. "I don't want noodles. I want something else. A burger or something."

I knew this was coming; I just didn't think it'd happen two weeks into dating.

Cooper's a social butterfly. I'm the exact opposite of that.

The first weekend we spent at home was perfect. There was nothing that could have ruined that high.

Last weekend, Cooper asked if I wanted to go down the street to the local sports bar with him to watch whatever football team always has him outraged.

I passed, and he stayed home with me.

I know he's getting antsy, being cooped up in the house. I can tell because I've had *The Vampire Diaries* playing for the last hour *and* he's rubbing my feet without me asking.

He definitely wants something.

"Do you want to grab dinner?"

And there it is.

"And I don't mean at The Gravy Train," he adds when I open my mouth.

Dammit. He knows me too well.

He reaches over and pulls my sketchpad down so I'm forced to look at him.

"We could go to Jack's Box. I know you like their fries," he says, batting those damn green eyes at me.

"Isn't the girl supposed to be the one to bat her lashes and get her way?"

"I'm sorry, did you just try to force gender roles on me?"

I pull my sketchpad back up, shaking my head. "Don't be annoying, Coop."

"I'm not annoying, just right. And starving." He squeezes my foot again. "What do you say? Want to go grab dinner at Jack's and then maybe a few drinks at Lorde's, do a little dancing? I know how much dancing with me turns you on," he teases.

"Is this your way of asking me to go out to drinks tonight with you and your co-workers?"

"Yes."

"And you're trying to woo me with food to get me to do that?"

"Yep."

"I really don't mind if you go by yourself. I trust you if that's what you're worried about."

"I'm not worried about that. I'm just worried about you sitting around here being lonely without me."

I lift a brow at him. "I've sat here plenty of nights without you, thank you very much."

A grin stretches over his lips, and I've known him long enough to know it's his *I'm having very dirty thoughts* smirk.

"What are you thinking about?"

"You...sitting around here without me." His grin grows. "I

bet you masturbated all the time when I wasn't here, didn't you?"

Warmth spreads through my cheeks, and he laughs.

I try to kick out of his grip, but it's no use. He holds me to him.

"What makes you think I don't still sit around masturbating when you're not here?"

"Oh, I bet you do. You're a total horndog. I would know." He winks. "Just say yes."

The idea of going out with him doesn't sound *that* awful. And we did have fun the last time we went out.

But this couch is also really comfy...

"What if I promise we won't leave the house the rest of the weekend?" he proposes. "Well, you have to leave for work. And so my other girlfriend can come over, of course. Can't have her here when you're here. That'd be awkward."

I kick at him and he laughs, grabbing my foot, halting my assault.

"Jack's Box does have amazing fries. And a burger sounds pretty good..."

"Good. Let's go grab some grub."

He shoves up from the couch in a hurry, taking me with him.

"*Oof.*" I land face-first on the floor, right by the pizza stain that won't come out of the rug.

"Why are you on the floor? Come on, I'm—"

"Starving. Yeah, I heard." I roll over and glare at him. "You know, you're kind of an awful boyfriend so far."

He grins. "That so?"

I nod. "The worst I've had, and that includes Bobby John."

He fake gasps and glowers at me as he lowers his body over mine, fitting against me and between my legs. "How dare you. You take that back."

I lift a shoulder. "Bobby John would never throw me on the floor."

He runs his nose up the column of my neck, peppering it with soft kisses as he makes his way to my ear, rolling his hips into mine. "I only threw you on the floor so I could ravish you."

"If this is what you call ravishing me, you have some work to do."

"Stop trying to get me to have sex with you," he says, nipping at my neck, making his way to my lips. "I'm trying to take you out on the town and show you off."

"No, you're just trying to get fed, especially because you know it's my turn to buy."

"Is it?" He shrugs. "I had no idea. But, I mean, if you insist…"

He seals his mouth over mine, stealing away all smartass comments I had lined up. He pushes his tongue past my lips, tangling it with my own, and we're lost in a heated kiss.

He rocks into me, his hard cock rubbing against my clit, the thin fabric of my sleep shorts leaving nothing to the imagination.

He trails kisses down my chin and over my neck. He bites at the swell of my breasts, moving swiftly down my body.

I'm so lost in the feeling building between my legs that I don't even notice what's happening until he hooks his fingers into the waistband of my shorts.

"Cooper…" I pant, rising up on my elbows, watching him. "What…what are you doing?"

He pulls my shorts and panties down my legs in one quick move, then peeks up at me.

"I told you." He grins devilishly. "I'm *starving*."

He disappears between my legs.

"ONE DRINK," I tell him as he pulls open the door to Lorde's, the loud music piercing my ears as soon as we step inside.

"Just one," he promises, his hand finding the small of my back as I walk past him.

Lacing his fingers with mine, he guides me through the lounge and steers me to the right. I see his co-workers back in the same corner they were in last time.

"Hey! Bennett made it!" Paul shouts when we approach, holding his hand out to Cooper. "Good to see you, man."

They clasp hands, giving them a few pumps. "Hey, man. How you been?"

I smile. It's the same exchange from the first time we came here, and I wonder if they always do this.

I've always liked Paul. Any time he's over at the apartment, he's polite and always tries to include me in whatever the guys are doing. That's a lot more than I can say for Cooper's other friends.

Paul slides his eyes my way, lifting his brows when he sees our hands interlaced, then grins back at Cooper. "Guess not as good as I could be." He flicks his gaze back to me. "Always a pleasure to see you, Caroline. Glad you came out to see us again."

I smile at him. "I was…convinced."

He tucks his lips together, bringing his beer to them. "I don't think I want to know the details of that." Then he tips the bottle back, taking a hefty swig. "Did you guys order drinks yet? I hope not, because don't forget we're making Eli pay. Put everything on his tab."

"Not yet, but now that you mention it, I am kind of thirsty." Cooper turns to me. "Want to grab a drink?"

I nod. "But—"

"Just one. Yeah, yeah, I heard you, you party pooper. Be right back," he says to Paul, then leads me through the crowd.

When we approach the bar, I'm surprised to find Calvin, the guy I danced with last time we were here.

"Babe!" he shouts, pushing off the bar when he sees me. "You came back for me! I knew you wanted some of this." His eyes trail over my body, taking in my outfit. He whistles, dragging his lip through his teeth like before. "Fuck, *babe*. You look good enough to eat, and damn am I hungry."

He reaches for me, and Cooper pulls me behind him, blocking the guy's advances and towering over him menacingly.

I've always known Cooper was tall, but I guess I didn't realize how tall until now.

This guy looks like a shrimp next to him. It's comical.

"Hands off," Cooper barks, his tone grisly and serious.

Calvin holds his hands up. "Hey, man. No harm." He looks over at me. "Want to call your dog off?"

Cooper's top lip curls, and I can tell he's getting madder by the second, the protective side that's always been there hitting a new high.

"Cooper, it's fine," I say, pulling on his arm. "I met him last time I was here."

"Cooper?" Calvin asks. "The best friend you allegedly aren't fucking?" He scoffs. "Right. Should have known. Dudes and chicks can never be *just friends*."

Cooper takes a step toward him, and Calvin shrinks back.

I giggle at how absolutely terrified he looks.

Calvin keeps his hands up, backing away, muttering something about how I probably wasn't worth it anyway.

Cooper looks down at me, brows raised. "You actually talked to that dude?"

I shrug. "You told me to mingle. I mingled."

"Guy is a tool."

"Tell me about it. It's especially funny because he's the one who ditched me. Last I saw him he was making out with some chick."

"What an idiot." Cooper shakes his head, leading us to the bar.

He lifts his hand when we find a spot, waving to a bartender on the other side. She shoots him a grin and makes her way down to us.

The closer she gets, the more familiar she becomes. I recognize the stunning blonde from the last time we were here.

"Hey, handsome," she drawls in an obvious *I want to sleep with you* tone. "What can I get for you tonight?"

"Hey, Shayla."

Cooper says her name with a familiarity I don't like one bit. That same fleeting feeling of jealousy I had when Maya talked about Cooper's lips zings through me again.

"I'll have my usual," he tells her. "And a spiced rum with root beer."

Shayla slides her eyes to me for the first time, and

recognition dawns. I'm sure she remembers the last time we were here and I was sitting in this same spot flirting with a different guy.

"Oh," she says quietly. "I didn't realize you were with someone tonight."

"Yep." Cooper slides his arm around my waist, pulling me closer. "This is my girlfriend, Caroline."

And there it is: the first time he's introduced me to anyone as his girlfriend and not just his best friend.

I wait for the surge of *Well, this is weird* to hit me, but it never comes.

It just feels natural.

That's how it is with him. Easy.

Almost like we don't have to try at all. We just ebb and flow together.

All my insecurities about Shayla dissipate as Cooper's eyes shine down at me with affection.

Cooper's past is his past, just like mine is mine. And none of it matters because nothing has ever felt this good before.

How could I have missed out on this feeling for so long?

"Well, in that case..." She slides her hand over the bar toward me, giving me a genuine smile. "Hey, Caroline. I'm Shayla. I work pretty much every Friday night and have been slinging drinks your guy's way for way too long now. He's mentioned you several times. It's nice to officially put a face with the name."

"Hi." I give her hand a shake. "It's great to meet you. I just hope he hasn't told too many embarrassing stories."

"None I'll ever repeat." She winks, then taps the bar. "I'll be right back with those drinks."

She hurries down the bar, and I turn toward Cooper.

"So," I say.

"So," he mocks.

"I take it you have a thing for blondes?"

He grins, like he knew I was going to say something about the girl he's obviously slept with before.

"Just one," he tells me. I lift a brow, and he shrugs. "She was brunette then."

I shake my head, grinning at him. "You're hopeless."

He leans down, pressing a kiss against my shoulder. "*Ly* devoted to you, *babe*."

"Here you go." Shayla slides our drinks across the bar. "I put it on Eli's tab. Paul said that's where all your drinks are going tonight."

She shoots us another smile before taking back off in the other direction.

"Are you guys really going to saddle Eli with the whole tab tonight?"

"Yep," Cooper says, taking a sip of his drink. "That asshole ruined over twenty hours of work this week all because he didn't back his crap up. We're pissed."

"Then why'd you invite him to drinks tonight?"

"So he could pay."

I laugh. "In that case, I may have more than one."

"That's my girl."

He clinks his glass to mine, and I take a hefty drink from my cocktail, the alcohol burning my throat on the way down.

Damn, Shayla must be making these things doubles because I instantly feel the booze go to my head.

We lean against the bar, looking out at the crowd.

We're quiet, and it's nice that we don't have to fill the

silence with meaningless chitchat. We're comfortable, and comfortable is nice.

"All right, ladies and gents and all non-binary folks!" someone says from the stage. "This is your final warning. We're starting our karaoke hour in ten minutes." They hold their hand over their eyes, scanning the room. "Who's going to be our first victim?"

"Right here!" Cooper shouts, pointing to me. A few heads turn our way, their stares burning holes through me. "This one! She wants to!"

"Cooper Bennett!" I try to hide behind him, but he's too big to move. "Stop it!"

"Come on, Care. Don't be shy. You have a great voice."

"I have an *awful* voice. You're always yelling at me when I sing in the shower."

"Because it sounds like there are at least three cats in there dying."

"And you want me to do that here? *In public?*"

"Yes. It'll be hilarious. Live a little."

"No, thanks." I set my drink down, turning for the exit.

He winds his arm around my middle, tugging me back to him, laughing into my ear.

"Nice try," he says as I wiggle out of his grasp. "You're not getting away that fast."

"I'm not singing either."

"How about this…if you sing, I'll sing."

"No."

"Fine. Will you sing if I sing?"

"That's the exact same offer."

He pushes his bottom lip out, batting his dark lashes at me for the second time tonight. "Please, Caroline."

I shake my head. "Uh-uh. No. You are *not* going to pull the batty lashes again."

"Why not? It totally worked last time."

"If you think your batty lashes are what got me here, you're wrong."

"Oh, right." His lips fall to my ear again. "Do you want me to eat your pussy again? Is that what this is?"

I flush, and this time not from embarrassment.

I squeeze my thighs together, that sweet burn his stubble left behind not letting me forget a moment of him being between them.

I want him again.

Bad.

"Stop," I hiss. "We're in public."

"Then let's go home."

"I thought you wanted to come out tonight? Drinking and dancing?"

"I want you more."

I laugh. "You act like you're sex-deprived."

"I am. Horribly so. You should probably suck my cock way more often."

"Like I said, hopeless."

"Like I said, hopelessly devoted to you."

I try not to grin, shaking my head.

Going home to have sex with Cooper—again—sounds amazing, but I also know he really enjoys his nights out, and I don't want him to give that up for me.

"Let's dance first," I say. "Then if you still feel like ravishing me after a few songs, we can go."

"Okay, but to be fair, I always want to ravish you."

We last one song.

Chapter 13

COOPER

MMM. Tits.

Monday mornings have slowly become one of my favorites.

Making Waves is closed, and if I work hard enough over the weekend while Caroline's at work, I can squeeze in a few hours with her just like this.

I give Caroline's boob a squeeze and she sighs, pretending to be annoyed at my early-morning advances.

I know she's awake, just like I'm sure, based on the boner I currently have, she knows I'm awake too.

"Are you pretending to sleep so you can fondle me and I can't get mad because you did it *in your sleep* and sleep you is at fault, not awake you?"

"Maybe."

She laughs, rolling over to face me. I feel her lips against the tip of my nose.

"Good morning."

I don't think I'll ever get used to this, waking up next to her. I can't believe I haven't always done it.

I peel my eyes open. "Good morning, trash breath."

"Oh my god," she growls, shoving at me. "You are so rude."

"What's rude is waking me up with your awful morning breath."

"I didn't hear you complaining about my awful morning breath yesterday. Or the day before."

"To be fair, the day before you woke me up with my cock in your mouth."

She blushes.

"You are so much dirtier in bed than I thought you were."

"I knew you'd thought about me in bed before."

She groans. "I swear, I'm sleeping in my own bed tonight."

She's a liar. She hasn't slept in her bed since the first night we had together.

That was over three weeks ago.

She's tried a few times, but she always ends up back in here, curled against me within a few hours.

"Whatever you say, trash breath."

She shoves me again and scoots out of bed, disappearing down the hall. I hear her scrambling around, then the water kicks on.

I crawl out of bed, stalking down the hall to the bathroom we share.

I push open the door and slide in behind her, reaching over her and turning off the water.

"Cooper!" she says, or at least that's what it sounds like. It's hard to tell with her toothbrush hanging out of her mouth, a dribble of toothpaste running down her chin.

"Quit running up my bills."

She spits, wiping the toothpaste off, glaring at me in the mirror. "The water bill is *my* bill."

"Yeah, but you get used to running this one up, you'll get used to running them all up." I cross my arms over my chest, leaning against the doorjamb. "I can't risk that."

"You're so annoying this morning." She rolls her eyes, resuming her brushing.

She knows I hate it when she does that. The defiance drives me fucking mad. Makes me want to bend her over this counter and show her it's not nice to roll your eyes at someone.

I lean into her, and she halts her movements when she feels me against her, feels how obvious it is that my cock is growing hard.

"Don't roll your eyes at me," I say into her ear, my eyes meeting hers in our shared reflection.

She lifts a brow, silently saying, *What are you going to do about it?*

I reach around her, pull the toothbrush from her mouth, and place it back in the holder.

I gather her wild hair into my hands, still damp from her after-sex shower last night, all while she stares at me with a flushed face and wide eyes.

"Spit," I tell her.

She does.

"Good girl." I release her hair. "Take your top off."

She strips the material off her body.

She's not wearing a bra, and my cock grows at the sight of her tits, which are marked with red spots from the time I spent paying them extra attention last night.

I press a hand against her back, urging her to bend over

the counter. I place open-mouthed kisses down her bare back as her breathing goes into overdrive.

Grabbing her wrists, I pull her hands behind her back, linking her fingers together.

"Don't move these," I tell her, squeezing her wrists in warning.

She nods, then gasps when I kick her legs apart.

I drop to my knees.

Curling my fingers into the waistband of her sleep shorts, I peer up, watching as she crushes her bottom lip between her teeth in anticipation of what's to come.

Slowly, I peel her shorts down her legs.

She's wearing a pair of lace panties that barely cover her cheeks.

Out of all the things that surprise me about Caroline, her wearing sexy-as-fuck matching bra-and-underwear sets is the most unexpected.

For some reason, I always pegged her as a plain white or cream-colored kind of gal.

I'm glad to know that after all the years, my girl can still surprise me.

My girl.

That's exactly what she is—mine.

She moans when I bite into her ass cheek, then run my tongue over the skin to soothe the sting. Who'd have thought buttoned-up, shy Caroline who's too embarrassed to talk about sex would be so into riding that pain/pleasure line?

She pushes back, wanting more.

I'm happy to oblige.

I nip at her again, all the way down her cheeks until I reach that sensitive skin where her ass meets her legs.

"Up."

Her eyes flutter open, brows creasing together.

I smack her ass.

"I said up. Tiptoes."

She pushes onto them, giving me the access I want.

Grabbing her cheeks, I spread her open and slide my tongue from her pussy all the way back to the hole I haven't yet had the chance to play with.

Her eyes fly open at the surprise contact, pupils dilated, and I can tell she likes it.

"Not yet," I tell her. "But soon."

She clamps down on her bottom lip again, liking the promise, then rises higher on her toes.

I take the invitation for what it is and run my tongue through her folds, plunging it into her core again and again until she's squirming against my face, needing more.

"Coop..." she murmurs, frustrated with my teasing. "More..."

"You want my cock or my mouth?"

"*Yes.*"

I slide two fingers into her pussy and suck her swollen clit into my mouth, pumping in and out of her at a hurried pace, running her right up to the edge, and then backing off just when I know she's about to explode.

"Ughhhh," she complains when I do it again. "*Please.*"

"Please what?" I say, pulling my mouth off her, slowing my strokes.

"Fuck me already."

I slip my fingers out, pull my pajama pants down just enough to free myself, and slide into her.

"Oh hell. *Fucking hell,*" I groan when she grips me tight. "Being with you…how the fuck did we wait so long, Care?"

"I-I don't know."

"You've ruined me, you know that? I'm ruined. Addicted. Completely fucking crazy for you."

She shudders at my words, a soft moan falling from her lips. "You've ruined me too."

I fuck her slowly, softly. Taking my time. When she tries to move her arms, I grab them, holding them firmly in place.

I lean down, dropping my lips to her ear. "Did I say you could move these?"

"N-No."

"That's what I thought."

She nods. "But, Cooper?"

"Hmm?" I ask, watching where we're joined, loving how my cock disappears inside of her like we're two puzzle pieces and fit together perfectly.

"I *need* to come."

"Do you now?" I ask, smirking.

Another nod. Another lip bite.

And I give in, fucking her…*hard.*

She cries out my name not even thirty seconds later, her pussy milking me into my own orgasm.

When the last of my shudders begin to subside, I collapse on top of her, pressing gentle kisses along her shoulder.

I let go of my hold on her and she sighs in relief, relaxing for the first time.

"You okay?" I ask softly. "I didn't hurt you, did I?"

She shakes her head. "No. I'd have told you long before now if you did."

"You promise?"

"Always."

"Good."

I kiss her one more time, then grab the condom to slide out of her.

I notice my mistake in that instant.

There's no condom.

"Shit," I curse, slipping out of her slowly.

Fuck. Shit. Fuck. This has never happened before. I've always been incredibly careful with protection, always very adamant about it. But something about Caroline turns me into a different person, one who's unable to control his urges.

"What?" she asks, pushing herself up and turning toward me. "What's wrong?"

"I was so eager to get inside you, I forgot the condom."

"It's okay," she says, sliding her arms around my neck at the same time I wrap mine around her waist. "I have an IUD and I trust you. We're good."

I nod. "I'm sorry."

"Don't be. I'd have stopped you if I were worried about it."

"Okay, but next time, I'll be more careful." I kiss the top of her head. "Let's get cleaned up."

We climb into the shower together, somehow making it out without fooling around too much, and head back to my bedroom.

"You want coffee?" she asks, pulling open my dresser and grabbing one of my shirts. She slips it over her head, forgoing underwear.

Seeing her in nothing but my t-shirt makes my cock twitch.

"Please. *Someone* kept me up late last night."

"*Someone* isn't even sorry about it."

She sticks her tongue out before heading for the kitchen.

I pull on a pair of boxer briefs, some sweats, and a t-shirt, my standard outfit for work. I'm just swiping on some deodorant when her phone buzzes against the bedside table, and I pad over to check to see who could be calling her this early.

Shit.

It's my moms trying to video-chat.

I swipe to ignore the call.

Not ten seconds later, my own phone starts to buzz, and I know it's them.

Dammit. I know if I ignore it, I'm going to get my ass chewed out like last time. Plus, it's suspicious as fuck if we both ignore their calls. The last time we did, they played twenty questions to see what the deal was.

I crawl onto the bed, reach across to the other table, and grab my phone.

"Good morning, pretty ladies," I say when their faces appear on the screen, flipping back around to a seated position. I rest my elbows on my knees, grinning down at them. "How are you?"

"Hey, favorite son," Momma Kira says, and I smile because I'm their only son. "We're good. Just wanted to catch you before you started doing all that tapping and clicking and whatever else it is you do on your computer all day long."

"Better not be looking at porn. Last time we talked with Caroline, she told us she caught you doing it again."

I chuckle because of course she did. "No porn, Momma."

"Show us your palms."

"Lydia!" Momma Kira scolds. "You leave that boy alone.

If he has hairy palms from masturbating too much, that's on him and I do *not* want to know about it."

"I just worry about him is all. He's so lonely out there in the wilderness."

"Just because I live in Colorado, doesn't mean I'm staying in some cabin in the woods," I interject. "I live in a metropolitan area. You'd know that if you came to visit."

"You know she hates flying," Momma Kira says, nodding toward her partner.

She rolls her eyes, but there's pure love in the gesture.

My moms met in college. They were roommates, and much like River and Dean, they loathed each other at first. It took them almost all of freshman year to warm up to each other.

Now, they can barely go twenty-four hours apart.

They're the reason I didn't do relationships.

If I couldn't have what they have, I didn't want it.

But now...

"Speaking of Caroline..." Momma Kira cuts through my thoughts. "How is our favorite gal doing?"

Just the thought of her makes my heart race. Sends a pulse of pure fucking elation right through me.

I can't remember the last time I felt this good, this whole.

This absolutely sure of something.

"You're smiling like crazy," Momma B says. "What happened?"

I am?

I try to school my features, not wanting to give away what's going on with us. We still haven't told our parents yet.

Just in case, as Caroline put it.

"There it is again," she comments. "Something funny?"

"Girlfriend of the year award goes to...drumroll, please... me! I bring coffee," Caroline announces, and I turn around to see her carrying two mugs, her eyes not leaving them as she tries to balance them in her hands without spilling anything. "Though I filled the mugs up too full. You're way better at this than I am." She shrugs, setting my coffee on the bedside table. "And that's fine. You have your skills and I have mine, like that thing I do with my tongue that you love. It's—"

Her eyes widen when she realizes I'm on the phone, mug paused halfway to her lips.

At least she put panties on.

"Oh god," she mutters.

I have to give her credit—she doesn't drop her cup.

But her face flames a bright red. Probably redder than I've ever seen it, and that's saying something.

I shake with laughter and she shoots narrowed, accusatory eyes my way.

"Cooper!" she hisses. "You could have warned me."

I shrug. "I wanted my coffee."

I turn my attention back to my moms. Momma Kira's smirking, and Momma B has her hand covering her mouth, probably trying to hide her laugh.

"Did I hear that right?" Momma Kira asks. "Girlfriend?"

I feel the corners of my lips pull up, still loving the fact that Caroline is indeed my girlfriend.

"Well," says Momma B, "guess that explains why he looks so happy. And here I was worried about his hairy palms."

Caroline sputters, nearly choking on her coffee.

No matter how long she's been part of my family, she still can't seem to get over how open and honest we are. My moms

182

have never been the type to shy away from talking about sex. They figured the more open they were, the more open I'd be, and the more I'd come to them with any questions or issues.

They were right.

"Don't hide behind him now, Caroline," Momma Kira teases. "Come say hi."

Caroline comes around the bed, taking the spot next to me, setting her own cup of coffee down, and cozying up at my side until we're both in the frame.

"Hey, Mommas," she says, giving them a shy grin. "I'd say it's nice to see you, but…"

They chuckle.

"So how long has this been going on?" Momma B asks, not wasting any time jumping to the twenty questions I'm sure are going to follow. "Oh no." She gasps, her hand flying to her chest dramatically. "You two weren't having sex in our house when you were here last Christmas, were you?"

"Momma!" I chide, and Caroline smashes her face to my shoulder, hiding from the camera. "No. Nothing like that. It's…new."

"How new?"

"A few weeks now."

"Four," Caroline answers, grinning against me, then finally looking at the phone. "We've been official for four weeks now. Well, almost four."

She's counting.

I fucking love that she's counting.

"Wow. A month and you didn't tell us?" Momma Kira sounds a little hurt, and I'm not surprised. I usually tell them everything.

"I didn't mean to lie. It's just—"

"It's my fault," Caroline interjects. "It's all such fresh territory and I didn't want to tell anyone, not knowing what was going to happen. We have too much history with each other and our families to bring anyone into it. I wanted to be cautious. *Just in case.*"

My moms exchange a glance, and it's one of those talking-without-speaking kind of moments.

I'd know—Caroline and I have them often.

"What?" I ask.

"It's… It's just…"

She pauses, chewing on her lip with uncertainty.

Momma B tilts her head, encouraging Momma Kira to talk.

She clears her throat.

"We just want you kids to be careful, you know? You've been best friends for a long time. Relationships are hard as it is, but adding in the fact that you two have known each other for so long… Well, we just hope you aren't rushing into anything and that you've really thought this through. Things are different now."

"We *do* definitely kiss a lot more."

The moms laugh.

"I'm sure you do," Momma B says. "Just…be careful. Be open. Communicate more now than you ever have. It'll save a world of hurt because there are things at stake now that weren't before."

"The heart," Momma Kira provides. "That's what's at stake now."

I want to tell her the heart was always at stake, but I understand where she's coming from.

Just in the last month, Caroline's come to mean more to

me than she used to. Hard to fathom, because she meant a whole hell of a lot to me before we started all of this.

Now though…I can't even describe the way she makes me feel. It's on a whole different level, and I've certainly never come close to feeling like this with anyone else before.

I nod and peek down at Caroline.

She's looking at me with eyes that say, *See? Just in case.*

I don't need a *just in case.*

I know what I want.

Her. *All* of her.

"We understand what you mean, Mommas," Caroline tells them, her eyes full of something I can't quite put my finger on. "We're being cautious."

They let out a relieved sigh, then Momma B leans toward the phone.

"And be careful in other areas too! Wrap your tool, Cooper Bennett. I don't want any grandbabies yet. I'm not old enough."

I laugh because she's about to turn sixty but has the spirit and energy of a twenty-year-old.

Caroline falls into a coughing fit, likely remembering that I was just inside her not even half an hour ago with nothing between us.

I squeeze her leg in a *Get it together* way.

"We'll be careful in that area too," I promise. "But, hey, I need to get working soon unless I want to answer to my boss as to why I haven't logged in for the day."

"Boo. Fine. Go be a grown-up and stuff," Momma B says, waving us away.

"Love you both!" Momma Kira blows us kisses.

"Love you too," Caroline and I say in unison.

We send a final wave before I press the *end call* button.

Caroline smacks at me before I even have the chance to turn my phone off.

"*Oh my god*," she hisses. "You could have told me you were on the phone! I just practically bragged to your moms about my oral skills."

"For what it's worth, you definitely have the right to brag. You're so good at suck—"

She slaps her hand over my mouth.

"Don't you dare finish that sentence."

I grin against her, pulling her hand away. "Or what?"

"Or I'll…I'll…"

"Suck my cock again?"

"Ugh," she complains, pushing my face away. She stands, shaking her head and heading toward the hallway, giving me a fantastic view of her ass. She stops at the door, peeking at me over her shoulder. "Seriously so annoying this morning."

Then, she rolls her eyes.

I chase her down the hall.

Guess work can wait after all.

Chapter 14

CAROLINE

"SO, I HAD AN INTERESTING MORNING," River says by way of greeting as she waltzes into Making Waves, coffees in hand like always.

We're just two days away from the Harristown Jubilee, and we're working around the clock to make sure everything runs smoothly during the event.

Maya's on advertising duty on top of running our normal online orders. River's working out inventory and keeping up stock. And I'm in charge of holding down the fort in the shop. I think River gave me the easy job because she's still holding out hope that I'll let her display my work.

"Oh, please tell me you found me an extremely hot and wealthy guy to date." Maya folds her hands together in prayer.

"Sadly, no. But if you happen to find a hot and wealthy guy who happens to have a brother, please send him my way. I'm about two hours away from kicking Dean to the curb."

Maya scoffs at her best friend. "Right. And I met Henry

Cavill yesterday." She pouts. "Dammit. Now I really wish I *had* met Henry Cavill yesterday."

"What'd Dean do now?" I ask.

"Breathed too loudly," she complains, but her lips pull into a grin anyway. "Fine. The bastard told me they ran out of cherry pie at The Gravy Train when he came back with coffee, but I was just there talking to Darlene and he's a damn liar. He lied about pie. Fairly positive that's a cardinal sin."

"Fairly positive you're being dramatic," Maya says, reaching over the counter to grab a coffee from the to-go tray.

"Was that your interesting morning?" I ask, grabbing my own coffee.

I already had one cup, but another might not be a bad idea with how much still needs to get done…and with how tired I am after Cooper kept me up *way* too late last night.

"Actually, no." River's lips curl into a mischievous grin. "My interesting morning started in the elevator when Mailbox Betty hopped on two floors below me. She had some remarkably noteworthy things to tell me."

"Mailbox Betty? Isn't that the busybody who won the pot about you and Dean dating and is always up in *everyone's* business?"

"Unfortunately," River pouts, remembering the building-wide pool Cooper and I may have taken part in. "But she actually had some good gossip this morning."

"Ooooh!" Maya claps her hands together excitedly. "I love good gossip. Lay it on us."

"There I was, minding my own business, when she starts telling me about the two horny neighbors she caught making out in the elevator car."

Oh no.

I sit up straighter, my heart beginning to hammer in my chest when I realize what she's getting at.

Crap, crap, crap.

Me and Cooper.

We're the horny neighbors.

Two nights ago, we walked down the street to grab dinner from The Gravy Train. On the ride down, I mentioned that I'd always wanted to be kissed romantically in an elevator like in the movies and my romance books.

He poked fun at me like he always does, and I didn't think about it again.

The moment we stepped on the elevator when we were headed back home, Cooper's lips were on mine. He pushed my skirt up around my waist, ripped a hole in my tights, and fingered me to completion right there in the car.

The thought of being caught made me come fast...and *hard.*

A blessing because when we reached our floor, Mailbox Betty was there waiting to catch a ride down. We were still kissing when the doors opened.

I blush at the memory, clenching my thighs together... realizing how badly I want to do it again.

I wonder if we'll always be like this, ready and eager to rip one another's clothes off no matter where we are.

I hope so.

"So, Caroline," River says, still grinning like a fool, "anything you'd like to share with me and Maya?"

Ugh.

Maya takes a sip of her coffee, then sputters when she realizes what River is getting at, coffee dribbling down her chin.

She wipes at the liquid, eyes wide as she stares at me in disbelief. "You and Cooper?" She smirks. "You dirty, dirty little secret keeper. How long?"

"Yeah, Caroline, how long?" River echoes.

I can't help it; a smile pulls across my lips just thinking about him. "A little over a month."

Maya gasps loudly. "You...you...you *hussy*! You've been sleeping with him that long and didn't say anything?"

I shrug, picking at the sleeve on my cup. "We didn't want to jinx it."

"And now?"

Another grin. "I think we're past that point."

"Awww." Maya clutches her chest. "That's actually kind of sweet. How'd it happen? Who jumped who first? Is he good in the sack?"

I laugh at her questions as she peppers me with them rapidly.

"You really are sex-deprived," I tell her.

"Trust me, I do not need the reminder." She frowns momentarily, probably thinking of the awful divorce she went through last year. Then she smiles again, waving her hand. "Anyway, give us the details. I want to know everything."

"Well, it happened not too long after you guys asked about our kiss."

"Ah," River says, nodding. "So *that's* why you canceled your date with the dude from the bookstore."

"That's why, and because I really don't think that would have worked out anyway. He was too shy for me. Which I know is ridiculous coming from me of all people, but I just realized I needed someone more...confident, and Cooper is *definitely* confident."

"I'm not going to pry into the intimate details of your sex life, but that truly sounds like he's deliciously confident in all the right ways in the bedroom."

She waggles her brows, and I giggle.

Gosh, I feel like I'm doing that so much lately. *Giggling.* Like a teenager who just fell in love for the first time.

Oh crap.

"I'm in love with Cooper."

The words hit my own ears, and everything clicks into place.

I am madly in love with Cooper Bennett.

My best friend since I was fifteen. The same guy who has been there through everything. The aftermath of my parents' divorce. All the embarrassing tribulations of high school. My first crush *and* my first boyfriend. He was there to hold me when my grandparents passed. When I lost my virginity to that asshole Bobby John. Hell, he moved halfway across the country just to go to college with me.

He's been there for all of it.

He's my rock. He's my person.

My *everything*.

River and Maya exchange a glance—then burst out laughing at the same time.

"We know," my boss says once they calm down.

"You do?"

Maya nods. "Yeah, it's kind of obvious. It's *been* obvious."

"It has?"

"For as long as we've known you, and you can believe me on that. I know something about repressed feelings," River tells me with a wink. "I've never seen two people so attuned to one another before. Whenever you're in a room together, it's like nobody else matters. You drift toward one another. You look at each other with this whole other level of understanding. Like he's your other half and you're his."

He is.

"I second all of that," Maya agrees. "I actually thought you two were dating for several months before River informed me you were just friends. I didn't believe her at first, because I just couldn't imagine how you *weren't* dating."

Now that I'm with Cooper, I can't imagine how it's possible either.

"Have you told him yet?" River asks.

I shake my head. "No. I mean, we've said it before, but that was…you know…"

"Before." She nods. "And that's completely different."

I've been thinking a lot about what his moms said, about how we need to be careful because there's a lot at stake between us now.

Our history and our hearts.

Before, losing Cooper would have been awful.

Now? Losing him would be completely devastating.

And I don't think I'd ever come back from that.

All I can do is hope he feels the same about me.

"That makes sense. I know I'd be scared as hell to fall for my best friend like that. Can you imagine if things didn't work out? You'd lose your boyfriend *and* your best friend all in one fell swoop. I mean, *yikes*. I—"

"Maya!" River hisses, nodding toward me in a clear *OMG shut up* gesture. "You are *so* not helpful."

Maya winces. "Oops." She shoots me a weak smile. "Just ignore me. I'm—"

"Right," I say. "I was just thinking it myself."

She places her hand on top of mine. "Well, don't, because it's pointless. You're Caroline and Cooper. Nothing is coming between you two. I just know it."

I hope she's right.

"Anyway, since I've already put you on the spot once this morning," River says to me, "have you thought about my offer?"

Have I thought about it? Only every day since she made it.

"Any decisions?" Her hazel eyes are hopeful, and even Maya looks excited.

I hate to disappoint them, but... "Not yet."

I have the confidence to make the designs and have been working on pieces over the past few weeks, but I lack that same courage when it comes to displaying them.

Playing pretend designer and seamstress in my bedroom is one thing.

Putting my work on display for the whole town to judge is another, and I'm not sure I'm ready for it.

River's shoulders deflate, but she recovers quickly. "Totally fine. Like I said, even if you come to me the morning of, you're in."

Maya bobs her head up and down vigorously. "What she said. And not to pressure you or anything, but I really hope you say yes. I've been wanting a top like the one you have on now since you first wore it."

"Thank you," I tell River again. "I'll—"

"Think about it. Yeah, I know." She winks. "All right, ladies. Let's get to work."

"WHAT'S WRONG?"

His question startles me, and I peek up at him from my position on his chest where I've been running my fingers through the hair there for the last ten minutes.

I should be in a blissful state considering Cooper just rocked my world *twice*.

But no matter how hard I try, I can't relax.

All I can think about is the fact that I'm in love with him.

And how much that absolutely terrifies me, especially since Maya's words have been circling in my mind all day.

I don't know what's going on with me.

Maybe I'm stressed about disappointing River because I plan to tell her I'm not putting my designs in the festival. Maybe it's my period that's supposed to start next week.

Or maybe it's that I've never been this wholly in love with someone before and it fucking terrifies me.

I try to play it off.

"What do you mean?"

He tucks a few loose strands of hair behind my ear. "I can hear you thinking. Something's wrong. What's going on?"

I sigh.

Of course I can't hide anything from him. He knows me too well.

"Do you think they're right?" I ask quietly. "Your moms and Maya, I mean."

"Maya?"

Crap.

"Uh, yeah," I say. "I kind of told River and Maya about us today. Well, technically Mailbox Betty told River in the elevator about what happened when *we* were in the elevator. She kind of cornered me about it this morning."

He chuckles. "Of course Mailbox Betty is telling everyone." He cups his hands around his mouth, then yells, "The old coot has nothing better to do than gossip!"

I swear I hear something bang against the wall.

"River and Maya know now?"

"Uh, yeah, is that okay?"

"Why wouldn't it be? If anything, it's kind of a relief. Now I can totally make out with you at The Gravy Train." He runs his hands through my hair, playing with it. "Is that what this is about? My moms and your friends knowing?"

"No. Maybe." I push off his chest, meeting his curious green eyes. "It's just...she said something similar to what your moms did. About what we're doing here, putting our friendship and hearts at stake."

A deep crease forms between his brows. "Okay...so?"

"Do you think we're making a mistake, Cooper?"

His face falls at my words.

"Come here," he says, grabbing my arm and pulling me up until I'm straddling his lap. He pushes that same errant lock behind my ear again. "Where is all this coming from?"

I shrug, not wanting to rehash my conversation with the girls. "Just thinking."

"Does it feel like that to you? Like we're making a mistake?"

"I...well, no," I tell him. "You?"

"Fuck no," he says, his voice strong. *Certain.*

He slides a hand up my cheek, cupping it and pulling until my forehead is resting against his.

"I'm scared. What if this doesn't work out? I don't want to lose my friend too."

"That's a moot point. I kind of like you and stuff."

195

I huff, annoyed by his non-serious answer.

"Look, Care, if you're asking if there's a chance this won't work out—sure there is. Just like there's a chance tomorrow won't come, or you won't remember to take the trash out because, by the way, it's your turn again."

I laugh. "Coop…be serious."

"I am. I am being serious. You're awful at remembering your trash-day duties."

I shake my head, pulling away from him. "You're ruining this."

"I'm not. I'm just trying to tell you there's nothing to worry about. Whatever comes our way, we'll be fine."

"You think?"

"I *know*. I mean, just look at us. You groped me and we thrived. Now we're having the best sex of our lives."

I sigh in exasperation, but a tiny smile pulls at my lips as I push out of Cooper's hold.

"I don't know what I was thinking hooking up with you."

"You weren't."

"I know."

He pulls me back to him, his lips brushing against mine. "But it was a good decision, yeah?"

The best. "Jury's still out."

"Really?" He kisses me, his hands sliding down my body to my hips, his cock growing hard against me as he drives his hips upward. My clit rubs against him, the friction making my already sensitive area pulse. "What can I do to help my case?"

"Hmm…I'm not sure."

"Well, I've got a few ideas…"

He slips inside of me and argues his case—rather convincingly.

Chapter 15

COOPER

"ARE YOU READY TO GO YET?"

"Almost!" she calls from her bedroom.

I toss my head back, sighing.

Here we are again: me waiting on her to get ready while she races around her bedroom telling me five more minutes... every five minutes.

"You're going to be late. You promised River you'd be at the store by nine AM sharp."

"Quit your complaining, Mr. Gets to Stay Home Longer!"

The girls are meeting at Making Waves to double-check inventory before heading over to the venue to start setting up. I have a few things to take care of with work, then plan to show up later for moral support and to make coffee runs.

"Come on, Care. I'm sure you look great. Plus, I'm sure you'd rather not piss off River by being late. Don't tell her this, but she kind of scares me."

I hear her laugh. "Just let me grab my shoes!"

Finally, I hear her making her way down the hall, and I rise up from the couch.

She steps around the corner wearing jeans that look like they've been painted on. A plum-colored sweater hangs off one shoulder, just waiting for me to sink my teeth into. Those same sexy-as-fuck boots she wore with her red dress complete the look, making me excited about peeling them off later.

"You look...*fuck*." I reach down, adjusting my hardening cock.

Her full lips curve into a coy smile, like she knows she's killing me right now. "I look *fuck*?"

"Mhmm. Are you sure you have to go today?"

She giggles as I close the distance between us, wrapping my arms around her waist.

"Yes, I'm sure."

I drop my lips to hers, kissing her breathless.

"Do we have time for a quickie?" I ask, pulling my mouth away, kissing up to her ear.

"Weren't you just complaining about me being late?"

Shit. I totally forgot. Caroline does that to me, short-circuits my brain.

I wonder if there will ever be a time she doesn't affect me like she does now. I sure as fuck hope not.

"Right." I nod, putting space between us so I don't get carried away. "You're right."

She laughs. "You're hopeless, Cooper."

"Hopelessly devoted." I wink. "You have everything?"

"Yep."

"Aren't you missing something?" *Like your designs?* I leave that out, but I know she's aware of what I'm asking.

I haven't pushed her about it again, but I've seen her working on new stuff the past few weeks. I know it's been for the festival.

Now she's standing before me empty-handed, and that doesn't sit right with me.

She shakes her head, her blonde curls bouncing. "No. I can't think of anything."

I sigh, pinching the bridge of my nose, growing increasingly exasperated.

She's not going to do it.

Again.

I *know* deep down she wants to design for a living. I know she wants to make something out of her passion. I can see it in her eyes that she wants to do this, and I know her well enough to be sure having her designs for sale would mean the world to her.

But she's going to turn River down because she's scared, just like she bowed to her father's wishes when she was too afraid to stand up to him.

"Seriously, Care?" I cross my arms over my chest. "What about all those pieces you've been sneakily working on the last few weeks? You're just going to pretend you didn't spend hours working on them? Pretend you don't want to do this?"

"I've always spent hours working on my designs," she contends. "That's nothing new."

I level her with a stare because I know she's lying.

Her hands come in front of her, and she wrings them together, nibbling at her bottom lip. "I can't do it, Cooper."

"Why not?"

She lifts a shoulder. "I'm...I'm just not ready."

I fight hard to hold back my groan. "You are. You're just fucking scared."

"Which means not ready."

"No. Not being ready would mean not having any pieces

done, and you do. You have plenty. They're hanging on the rack in your room. Being scared is just that—being too chicken to take a chance."

"Fine!" She tosses her hands in the air. "I'm scared, okay? Absolutely terrified to fail and realize my father was right all along and this is nothing but a hobby for myself, not something I can make a living from. But so what? It's *my* choice."

"Well, it's a dumb choice."

She sighs. "I have things to focus on today—like making this a successful event for Making Waves—that are a lot more important than putting some silly, homemade designs that likely won't even bring in any cash up for display."

I grit my teeth, frustrated with her for being so flippant about what she works so hard on. Like it doesn't matter, even though it makes her happy.

"Can we drop this?" she asks, tossing her hair over her shoulder, looking fed up with this conversation. "I'm going to be late, and I don't have time to argue about this."

I'm fed up too.

Fed up with her running away and hiding behind her fears.

I'm over her believing she's not allowed to have a dream and go after what she wants.

"Coop?" she urges. "Promise me you'll respect my decision on this?"

I make a noncommittal sound, but it's not enough for her.

She sighs again, crossing her arms over her chest, and I know she won't leave until she hears me say it.

"I promise." But I know it's a lie as soon as the words drop from my lips. I have no intention of letting her run from such a huge opportunity. "I'll drop it."

"Thank you." She presses a kiss to my cheek. "I'll see you in a few hours?" I nod. "Good. I really do have to go now, or I'll be dead, and you're not the only one River scares."

She gives me another kiss, then disappears out the door.

I stare after her, frustrated as hell.

She's talented. She *deserves* what River is offering her. I just wish I could shake some confidence into her and make her see that.

"Screw it," I say, making my way to her bedroom.

If she won't take initiative in making her dreams come true, I will. She might be upset at first, but when she sees I'm right and sells out like I know she will, she'll forgive me.

She needs someone to push her. I'll be that person for her.

I'll be damned if I sit on the sideline and watch her let this pass her by.

EVERY YEAR the city shuts down the entire one-hundred-acre park for the jubilee, the biggest event of the year. Somehow, already, this one feels bigger than all the others, and it doesn't even officially kick off for another thirty minutes. I swear several hundred people are milling about already.

"Hey, man," Dean says, walking up to me. "Nice sweater."

"Shut up, asshole," I mutter, noting he's wearing his standard weekend attire of jeans and a faded band tee. "Caroline made me wear it. *Dress nice but not too nice*, she said."

201

"And you went along with that shit?" He shakes his head, taking a drink of his coffee. "Someone's pussy-whipped."

Guilty as fucking charged.

"Whatever," I tell him. "Does The Gravy Train have a truck here? I didn't even think about stopping to grab a coffee on the way. I could use one right about now."

He nods toward the direction he just came from. "No, but I passed at least ten trucks on the way over here."

"Meh," I say. "That's not the same."

"Why do you think I grabbed one before coming here?" He takes another sip. "So, how's it going in there?"

"Not sure. They've already rearranged things twice since I've been standing here, and it's still 'not right,' as River keeps saying."

"Again? They did it twice when I was here helping them set up. I thought they had it all planned out already—River hasn't been able to shut up about it for weeks."

"Tell me about it. When Caroline and I aren't—"

"Having wild, wild sex?" he interrupts, smirking.

I laugh. "Yeah, that. When we aren't *preoccupied*, it's all she's talked about, making sure everything is perfect and in place."

"Did she change her mind about her display?" I shake my head, and Dean frowns. "Damn. River was really rooting for her. Sucks, because from the way River tells it, your girl is mad talented."

She is.

And when I get the chance to talk to her, she'll realize she *needs* to do this.

I know she will.

"Well, since they're still in there working, I'm going to take a walk around and scope out the competition, see who I can charm over this way," Dean says.

"Is that your role in all this?"

"Yep. Want to join?"

"Sure." I shrug. "I have nothing better to do. But first, I need some caffeine. I'm going to head that way," I say, pointing the way he came from, back where all the food trucks are. "Find some coffee. Then I'll catch up with you."

"Sounds good."

He takes off to scout things out, and I start toward the caffeine. I stop at the first truck I find, not caring who it is, and place an order for two black coffees.

One is for me, and the other I'll use to try to entice Caroline when I give her my big speech.

She needs to get out of her own head and realize she's talented, realize we're not all just blowing smoke up her ass and her "silly, homemade" designs are worth more than she gives herself credit for.

When she sees how right I am, how much I believe in her by bringing her designs, I know she'll see I'm right.

"Here you go, sir," the kid in the truck says, handing over my coffees.

"Thanks." I tuck a few bucks in his tip jar.

Fresh brew in hand, I make my way back toward the other end of the strip, feeling excited. This is about to be a damn good day because Caroline's dreams are going to come true, and I'll be part of that.

There's a shout in the distance, and I look up to see someone frantically waving her arms.

It's River.

I speed up to get to her.

"What's up?" I ask when I'm within distance.

"Oh, good. Coffee." She grabs a cup from my hand, taking a big gulp from it, not caring that it wasn't for her. Whatever. She looks like she needs it anyway. "The box, the one sitting behind the counter at the shop—did you put it in the truck last night when we were loading up?"

Oh shit.

I completely spaced on it. River asked me to grab it no less than three times, and I was too busy being distracted by how Caroline's ass looked every time she bent over and how badly I wanted to push her skirt up around her hips and drive into her.

"Ugh," she groans, all the hope in her eyes draining. "I'm guessing by the lack of color in your face, you didn't." I shake my head. "Shit, shit, shit. That's why nothing is looking like the diagrams I drew up. I left a much-needed chunk of my inventory at the shop, and there's no time to go grab it." Hands on her hips, she begins pacing back and forth in front of me. "The chamber of commerce dude is set to finish his speech soon, and that's when things are going to get really nuts in here, not to mention the traffic you'd have to endure."

"Fuck, River." I blow out a breath. "I'm such a moron."

She waves off my words as the truck door opens and Caroline pokes her head out, taking in River's worried strides.

"Hey," she says softly, approaching us. "No luck?"

"No," River says. "It's my fault for not putting it with the other boxes. I was hoping you would change your mind. I was saving that spot for you and set that box aside just in case."

Oh, fuck.

This is *perfect*. This is my chance to get Caroline's work on display.

"Caroline has pieces in my car."

Her head whips toward me, and I can feel her angry eyes boring into me.

"I can go grab them," I offer, willing myself to not look at her.

"You brought them?" River asks Caroline, hope lighting up her face.

Caroline's eyes dart back to me, and I can see she's torn between helping her friend and wanting to murder me for putting her on the spot.

She might be mad at me now, but she needs the push. She'll never go anywhere with the one thing that brings her joy if she keeps turning down opportunities like this.

If it makes me the bad guy for wanting her to be genuinely happy, I'll wear that name tag.

She drags her eyes back to River. "Apparently."

"Can we sell them?"

"I—"

"Please, Caroline. Please. I'm in a bind here. If you're worried about the money aspect of it, don't. I'll cut you a check as soon as we get back to the shop."

"It's not the money," Caroline says. "It's…other things."

"Look, you're nervous—I get it. I was nervous too when I took a chance on starting my own business. But if I hadn't taken a chance on it, I wouldn't be here today. *You* wouldn't be here today. Sometimes you just have to have a little faith that things are going to work out and go for it."

Caroline brushes a curl behind her ear, her nerves loud and clear, but I also see her wavering just the slightest bit.

River folds her hands together, tucking them under her chin, begging Caroline with her eyes.

Please, she mouths.

And Caroline caves.

"Okay."

"Yes!" River wraps her in a hug, squeezing her tightly. "Oh my gosh, *thank you*! Thank you, thank you, thank you!" She releases her, clapping her hands. "This is so huge! You just saved us so big."

Caroline shoots her a shaky smile.

"You." River points to me. "Go get the stuff. We still need to put everything on hangers and set up displays and— whatever. You don't have to know all the details. I just need them ASAP, so run."

I nod, and she turns away, muttering about everything she still needs to do.

She disappears into the truck, leaving me alone with Caroline.

She turns to me, and I see it.

It's written on her face clearly.

Betrayal.

She's hurt.

And I fucking hate when she hurts.

A pang I wasn't expecting hits me square in the chest.

"Hey! Come on, Caroline," River says, poking her head back out of the truck. "We need to get this stuff moved around."

Caroline turns to go, and I reach for her.

"Care…" I say, grabbing her wrist.

She pulls out of my grasp, shaking her head. "Just go, Cooper."

She leaves me standing there without another word. Not even a backward glance.

And I know in that moment that I fucked it all up.

Chapter 16

CAROLINE

HE LIED.

Cooper lied to me, and I can't stop thinking about it. Even as the day rolled on and we got busy with the event, I couldn't push it out of my mind. It was all I could focus on. I was moving through the festival like a robot.

There hasn't been a time in our friendship when he hasn't been completely honest with me. I know this because I know *him*. We've always been able to trust each other wholly…until now.

He said he'd drop it. He said he'd let me work through my fears on my own. Said he'd respect my decision.

And he didn't.

Cooper lied to me.

"You sold out."

River's words snap me from my fog.

"Huh?"

"You. Sold. Out."

"I…did?"

She nods enthusiastically. "All of them. Gone. I just did the count. Checked it three times. Congrats, you're officially a sellout!"

Cooper occupied my mind so much today, I paid little attention to my designs on display. Didn't fret over it. I thought for sure when River started hanging my stuff on the rack, I'd have a panic attack, but nothing came. I was too busy trying to figure out how a man who's never once lied to me before could suddenly do it so effortlessly. How he could betray me without flinching.

But hearing that I sold all thirty pieces? For the first time today, I feel something other than the dull ache in my chest.

I was so scared I'd fail if I put myself out there that I never really considered flourishing, and that's exactly what happened.

"See?" she says, bumping her shoulder into mine. "I said you'd kick major ass, didn't I?"

I blush. "You did."

"And can you believe that lady bought *six* pieces?" Maya squeals, giddy about the day. "That's like a whole wardrobe! We killed it!"

In addition to me selling out, we sold over half of our inventory and got a ton of foot traffic with promises to visit the full shop.

"We really did, and I'm so proud of us," River says. "But I just have to say, we owe so much of today's success to the lady of the hour…" She looks right at me when she says it. "I have no doubt it was your display out front that encouraged so many to come into the truck."

"No way," I argue. "It was a group effort."

"Sure, but we couldn't have done as well as we did if we didn't have such a strong attention grabber. *You* attracted those sales. *Your* designs did that. You totally saved us last minute."

"We'd have done amazing even without that."

"Stop arguing and just be proud, dammit!" She laughs, then reaches across the counter and squeezes my hand. "Because I sure am. I'm thankful you took a chance and put yourself out there. I know it was hard for you to do, but I'm beyond grateful."

"Ditto," Maya says, nodding and smiling.

"*Now* do you believe me?" River says. "You totally killed it. You deserve a spot in the store full time."

I balk, and she laughs.

"Okay, okay. Maybe you aren't ready for that just yet, but what about putting a few pieces up on the website? I was thinking of launching them next month for our anniversary."

"Next month? Already?"

"Hell yes already. I want to keep this momentum going, baby. I don't want to chance you losing your confidence and changing your mind. You're on fire—let's keep it that way."

I *am* feeling good... "How many are we talking?"

"Hmm...let's say five styles? Various sizes on each, of course. Is that doable?"

I grin. "I think I can do that...although, you know, I *do* have a full-time job and my boss is a little bit of a hard-ass sometimes."

"Yay!" She claps her hands together. "We'll talk logistics on Tuesday, get a contract hammered out and whatnot. Oh! Speaking of..." She shuffles through the various binders in front of her, pulling out a financial one. She scribbles on a check, then rips it out and hands it my way. "Your commission."

My throat constricts as the check slips into my grasp.

Tears begin to well in my eyes, but I blink them away, not wanting to cry in front of them.

This is it. The first real proof that this hobby of mine could be something more.

It's…exhilarating.

And for the first time, I think I might actually be able to do this.

I give them both a wobbly smile, unable to form words right now.

She clears her throat. "So, I don't know about you two, but I'm wired and exhausted all at once. I don't think I'm going to be able to sleep at all tonight—not that that's different than any other night though." She shrugs. "I just really hope Dean isn't asleep when I get home because celebration sex sounds *really* good right now."

"Ugh." Maya groans. "I'm so not jealous at all. You get to go home to Dean. Caroline gets to go home to Cooper. Me? I'm going home to…well, my kid who keeps texting me asking me when I'll be home because he's hungry and still can't figure out how not to ruin mac and cheese."

"My nephew," River says, shaking her head. "So pitiful."

"He got it from you," Maya insists through a yawn. "Well, ladies, that would be my cue to get my old ass home." She grabs her purse from the counter, slipping it over her shoulder. "Celebratory breakfast in the morning? The Gravy Train at eight?"

River pins her with a stare. "Are you going to show up at eight? Or roll in late again?"

"I guess we'll see, won't we?" Maya presses a kiss to River's cheek. "Good job today, babe."

"Couldn't do it without you," River replies as they wrap their arms around each other in a hug.

Maya rounds the counter my way, holding her arms out to me. "Come here." She pulls me into an embrace just as fierce as the one she gave her best friend. "I'm so, so incredibly proud of you. And I want to place an official order for one of those blanket tops, okay? I look really good in blue."

I squeeze her back, laughing. "You got it."

She releases me, then sends us a finger wave as she disappears out the door.

"Why don't you head out too?" River says to me. "I can finish running the numbers and then I'll close up shop. Go home and celebrate with your man."

"I'm fine. I don't want to leave you here alone."

"Suit yourself."

She shrugs, burying her face back in her books, not noticing that I'm avoiding going home.

I'm not ready to face Cooper yet, because I don't know what I'm going to say to him.

He's who I want to celebrate my victory today with, not just as my boyfriend, but also as my best friend.

Except I can't.

And it reminds me all over again of what Cooper's moms and Maya warned of, losing my boyfriend *and* my best friend because we didn't think this through.

Did we make a mistake?

"Fine. You convinced me," she says not even five minutes

later, pushing the books aside and closing them. "I'm leaving too. Besides, I'm beat. I could use a bath, a glass of good whiskey, and a slice of pie, which I know Dean totally picked up for me. I have him trained well."

She winks, and I laugh because we both know she doesn't have Dean trained to do anything other than throw all her sass right back at her.

"Plus, I'm sure Cooper is just dying to celebrate with you." She bounces her brows.

I'm sure that's the exact opposite of what Cooper's waiting for.

As much as I avoided him today, he did the same to me.

He knows I'm upset. He knows I'm hurt.

He knows he screwed up.

Just like I know I'm going to have to face him eventually.

"Come on." She reaches across the counter for her purse, then ushers me toward the door. "Let's walk back together and talk about what I need to do to convince you to have a permanent spot in the shop."

I TOLD River I wanted to grab something at The Gravy Train for dinner, and I was thankful she was too excited to get home to Dean to think much of it and went ahead without me.

I don't need anything other than a moment to breathe and think before facing Cooper.

I pull the door open and step into the quiet diner, letting the familiar scent of pie wash over me.

It's comforting, and right now I could go for some comfort.

"Hey, kiddo," Darlene says when I walk up to the counter. "Why the long face? I heard you ladies did great at the festival today. You should be smiling, not frowning."

"You heard about that? How?"

"I keep up on my favorites." She smirks. "Plus, Dean stopped by earlier to get pie for River."

She curls her lips at the mention of Dean, and I try to hide my laugh at her contempt toward him. She still hasn't forgiven him for making River upset.

"What can I get for you tonight, dear?"

"Do you happen to have any fresh coffee?"

Her brows shoot up. "Coffee? For you? This late?"

I nod. "Please."

I have a feeling it's going to be a long, sleepless night anyway. What's one more coffee going to hurt?

A frown pulls at her lips. "I don't mean to pry, but whatever's going on between you and that handsome boyfriend of yours, you'll work it out."

"What do you mean?"

"Come on, I was a young gal once, and I had plenty of boy troubles in my day. I'm going to assume he did something really dumb."

I nod.

She huffs, resting her elbows on the counter. "Figures. He's been spending too much time with Dean. That boy's brand of stupid was bound to rub off on him a little."

I snicker.

"What did he do?"

I give her a rundown, and she gasps.

"That beautiful, beautiful dumb boy." She tsks. "I don't blame you for being mad. Heck, I'm mad *for* you."

I smile. "Thanks, Darlene."

"Of course. Us girls have to stick together." She winks and pats my hand. "Listen, I know this is a shitty situation, but for what it's worth, I've seen the way Cooper looks at you—and I don't just mean since you two finally pulled your heads out of your butts over a month ago. For as long as you two have been coming here, I've seen it. He looks at you like you're his everything. That boy is madly in love with you."

Love?

I can't help but feel if that were the case, he wouldn't have done what he did today.

"Did that thought not cross your mind?" Darlene asks, drawing my attention back to her.

Well…no.

I mean, I hoped, but what girl doesn't?

Her lips turn up at the corners when I don't answer. "You love him, don't you?"

"So much," I whisper.

"You tell him that?"

"No. It's…complicated."

She grunts. "It always is."

"Have you ever fallen in love with your best friend only to have them lie to you and break your trust?"

"Well…no, I haven't. I guess that does complicate things a bit, huh?"

I pinch my fingers together. "Just a bit."

"Sorry, kiddo." She winces. "Tell you what, coffee is on me tonight. You sound like you really do need it."

"Thank you."

She tosses me another wink, then pours me a fresh cup of

joe. She slides the coffee my way and gives me a somber smile before moving away.

Coffee in hand, I take the long way home.

When I finally make it up to our apartment, Cooper's light is off.

And for the first time in over a month, I sleep alone.

Chapter 17

COOPER

FOR THE FIRST time in my life, I was really starting to love Mondays.

Lazy mornings in bed with Caroline. The laughter. The fun. The sex.

But Caroline didn't come to my bed last night, which makes it two nights in a row she's slept in her own room.

I've reached for her only to find nothing but miles between us so many times I've lost count.

The only real communication we've had is a note that read, *Give me time.* It was sitting next to the full coffee pot the morning after the festival.

It feels like it did in the days after I kissed her. She's not actively avoiding me this time and running from the room every time I walk into it, but we're not talking either.

We're sharing the same space, but we're not.

It's too quiet and feels like, at any moment, something— or someone—is going to explode. It's so fucking hard to breathe because I feel like all my reasons to do so are missing.

I had to get out of there. Had to get a break from the silence.

Which is how I ended up in front of The Gravy Train, trying to convince myself to go inside and not storm back to our apartment and demand she talk to me.

"Hey, man." I turn to find Dean striding up to me. It's early, and based on his attire of dress shirt and slacks, he's headed to work. "You going in or coming out?"

"In."

"Coffee? I'm headed in for some breakfast."

I'm not sure I'm up for company, but I don't really want to be alone right now either.

"Sure," I say, pulling the door open.

"Don't tell River," he starts as he walks in ahead of me, "but I come here sometimes during the week without her so I don't have to share my pie."

I chuckle. Probably smart. River is profoundly serious about her pie.

"Oh hell," Darlene grumbles as we approach the counter. "Who let you two in here?"

Dean smirks at her. "Hey, sugar."

She rolls her eyes. "Please, boy. You're young enough to be my kid. Don't try that flirting stuff with me."

Dean laughs. "Two coffees, please. And I'll take whatever cherry pie you have left."

"For you or River?"

"Is that going to decide whether you have any pie or not?"

"Maybe."

"River, then," he tells her. "We're still celebrating this weekend's accomplishments. They're already seeing the results of all the foot traffic over the weekend."

I left before the festival ended. It was obvious Caroline didn't want me there. Every time I tried to talk to her, she shut me out.

So, I left.

I still have no idea how it ended up working out for her. I've wanted to ask so many times, but it never feels right.

God, I don't even want to think about how she walked around the festival looking like an automaton on what was supposed to be a joyful day for her, displaying her work for the first time.

It turned into anything but, and it's all my fault.

I crossed boundaries I shouldn't have. Pushed her when I promised I wouldn't. Went behind her back intentionally.

I *lied* to her. I *deceived* her.

I'm a fucking asshole.

"Pfft." She waves her hand. "I knew they would. That little boutique of theirs is adorable and they work so dang hard on it. I had no doubt they'd rock it." She punches a few buttons on the register. "Since it's for River, I'll see what I can scrounge up."

She scurries off to the back, and Dean shakes his head.

"It's messed up they love River more than me," he complains as we make our way to our regular spot.

"I think Darlene's still mad at you for moving out of River's apartment."

"I moved back in!" he argues as we sit down. "We've been together for months. You'd think she'd be over it by now."

"Yeah, man, but girls love to hold grudges. Trust me."

I try not to focus too hard on that reality given my situation.

I don't want Caroline to hold a grudge. I want to talk to her. Want to explain my side.

But she requested time, and this time, I'm respecting her wishes.

I've learned my lesson.

"Man, my feet are still killing me from walking around this weekend. I can't imagine how the girls are feeling. Bet they're glad the shop is closed on Mondays so they can recuperate. Probably tired as fuck, especially after having to run the shop yesterday and the continued...*celebrations* last night." He grins impishly. "If you catch my drift."

I wouldn't know. There was no celebrating.

Just...cold.

"Here are your coffees," Darlene says, appearing at the end of the table with our coffees and Dean's pie. "And a little something extra for you." She sets a chocolate chip cookie on the table. "You look a little down this morning."

I try to muster a smile, but it's a weak one.

She pats me on the back. "I'll be at the counter if you boys need anything else."

I stare down at the cookie I usually love to treat myself with and feel queasy just looking at it.

I push it away.

"You're turning down free treats?" Dean points down to it, and I shrug. "May I?"

"Go for it," I tell him, wrapping my hand around my coffee and taking a healthy swallow.

"So," he says after devouring half the cookie in one bite. "What'd you do?"

I furrow my brow. "What do you mean?"

He levels me with a *Don't play dumb* look.

I sigh, scratching at the stubble on my face. "I think I messed up with Caroline."

"Well, by your sulking and hers, that much is obvious. I'm going to assume it has something to do with her designs just showing up at the last minute."

I nod and sink lower in my chair, crossing my arms over my chest. "I'm a complete idiot."

He laughs. "If it makes you feel any better, River always thinks I'm a complete idiot and we're still doing fine."

I shake my head. "No, man. This one is... It's big. I messed up royally."

He tilts his head, chewing the rest of the cookie, waiting for me to explain.

I tell him what happened with Caroline's father and how she started viewing her work differently because of it. How his lack of approval somehow invalidated what she did and she never thought she could pursue a career in design. Then I tell him about our conversation on the morning of the jubilee.

"She specifically asked me to drop it, and I promised I would."

"But you couldn't," he guesses, digging into his pie next.

"Fuck no. She's so busy hiding behind her fears that she doesn't realize what an incredible break River is handing to her. This could open so many doors, could give her a chance to take what she loves to do and make it more than a hobby." I heave a sigh. "I've been watching her yearn for this for ten years, and I've watched her push her own dreams aside for the same amount of time. I can't keep letting her do that to herself."

He nods. "I can understand how that'd be frustrating."

"It is. Incredibly."

"So, what'd you do, then?" His eyes widen as he plays it out in his mind. "Shit. You totally brought her stuff anyway and offered it up to River without permission, didn't you?"

I grimace. "Maybe."

He takes another bite of his pie, shaking his head. "Dude."

"I know."

"That's...*dirty*."

I hate that he uses that word, but it's so fucking fitting for how I feel.

I wish I could take it back.

The betrayal in her eyes...it fucking gutted me.

I've had this pit in my stomach all morning. Not even my coffee tastes good.

"She has to be pissed at you. I know I would be." His words don't make me feel any better. "What the hell were you thinking?"

I blow out an exasperated breath. "I was giving her the push her father took away."

"And was that *your* call to make?"

"I just...I saw how badly she wanted to do it but was too scared. I thought of all the times she almost took control of what she genuinely wanted, and then all the times she's backed away. I thought if I brought them along and she saw how great the truck was doing, she'd be more open to adding her stuff into the mix. Then the box was lost and..."

"You volunteered her as tribute," he finishes. He takes a sip of his coffee, then sets the mug down. "So, what are you going to do?"

"Grovel?"

"That's a start." He chuckles. "Have you talked to her at all?"

"Not since the festival. She's been…distant."

"Can't say I blame her."

"Me either. It was a total dick move."

"Look," he says, setting his fork down. "For what it's worth, I can see why you did what you did. I can't say I'd do the same with River, mostly because she'd castrate me and I'm terrified of her, but I get it. I think if you explain your side, she'll come around. And if she doesn't, well, I guess you can sleep on our couch tonight. But don't tell River I invited you. That'll get me in trouble, and she'd accuse me of choosing sides. Just show up looking all pitiful and shit."

I snort. "Thanks. I appreciate it. I just hope it doesn't come to that."

"For your sake and mine, neither do I. So you better sack up and tell the girl you love you're sorry and will never do it again."

Wait…the girl I *love*?

Am I in love with her?

No way. It's too soon…isn't it?

Then again…it's Caroline.

Nothing with us has ever made much sense.

"Wow. You should see the fucking grin on your face right now," Dean taunts. "I've seen that look before."

"What look?"

"*Love.*"

"What?"

"L-O-V-E." He nods, grinning. "Oh, yeah. You're totally in love with her."

I shake my head, ready to argue. "I'm—"

Totally, completely, abso-fucking-lutely in love with her.

"Oh fuck."

He laughs. "Just now realizing it?" I nod. "Yep, been there. Sneaks up on you, huh?"

I'm not some hopeless romantic who wishes on the clock when it's 11:11 or whatever, but I'm not a cynic either.

I figured I'd fall in love one day. I guess I just never thought it would be with Caroline.

But now that it's right here in front of me, I can't believe I didn't see it before.

I'm in love with her...and I think I always have been.

I blow out a breath. "What the hell am I going to do?"

"What do you mean? You tell her."

"What?" I balk. "I can't tell her that."

"Why not?"

"Because she's...*Caroline.*"

"And?"

"She's my best friend."

Another laugh. "It's a little late for the *just friends* bit, huh?"

"No. I mean, it's obvious we're more than just friends, but...shit. It's one thing to sleep with someone and have feelings for them. It's another thing entirely to sleep with them and fall hopelessly in love."

What if she doesn't feel the same?

What if, especially after what I did, she thinks we made a mistake?

What if she can't forgive me?

"Listen, man, I've seen you and Caroline together for a while now, right? Well, not to get all mushy and shit, but I can't ever imagine stumbling upon two people who are better suited for one another. And that includes me and River, mostly because we're a horrible idea together." A lovesick

224

grin stretches his lips because he knows that's not true. "You have nothing to lose telling her you love her."

Except her.

I can't lose her, and I don't just mean because we're dating.

I'd be losing my best friend too.

That scares me more than her telling me she doesn't feel the same way.

I *have* to tell her.

"How'd you tell River?" I ask.

He twists his lips up. "Trust me, you don't want advice from me on how I told her. We weren't even on speaking terms and I just blurted it out when she was mad at me—again —for playing my music too loud."

I laugh. "You do kind of have shit taste in music."

He glowers at me. "I'll let that slide, but only because you're having an existential crisis right now." He pushes his empty pie plate away. "Well, I need to get going. Guess I have to go teach little heathens some English."

"Good luck with that."

He stands, tossing a couple bucks onto the table for Darlene. "I'll leave you with this thought: I almost lost River once, and it fucking sucked. I get what you're going through. Just…make her listen."

Chapter 18

CAROLINE

SIX.

That's the number of days it's been since I've spoken to Cooper.

The number of days it's been since I've touched him. Kissed him.

And the number of days I've been nursing a broken heart.

There's so much I want to say to him, but I'm still angry. Still hurt. The last thing I want to do is say something I'll later regret.

It's been difficult being in the same apartment as him, treading carefully around him and his stares.

Because if he thinks I don't know he's looking at me, he's wrong.

I can feel his eyes on me, like he's caressing me with his hands. Reaching right into my soul.

There have been moments I've wanted to knock on his door and tell him what an ass he is just as many times as I've wanted to tell him I love him.

But I don't.

All those feelings of anger and fear bubble back up and I back away.

The worst part? Over a month ago, he would have been the first person I'd run to talk to.

Not anymore.

"Hey."

River pulls me from my thoughts as she slides up to the checkout counter I've been sitting behind all day. With my sketchpad laid out in front of me and a pencil in my hand, I'm still technically working. Not moving much, but working.

I lift my head. "Hey."

"God, you look awful. You want to day-drink in the back office and talk shit about boys? I'm sure Dean's done something dumb this week I can bitch about for a while."

I bark out a laugh, not surprised. "You have booze back there?"

"Are you kidding me? Do you know how many late nights I've had here? Of course I have booze stashed." She winks. "So, what do you say? Couple drinks to drown your sorrows?"

"Thanks," I tell her. "But I'm okay."

She frowns, something she's been doing a lot lately.

I came clean about what Cooper did at the festival on Tuesday when River again hinted at putting up a display in the store. She felt awful for putting me on the spot, not knowing Cooper went behind my back and lied to me about staying out of it. I keep telling her it's fine and not her fault, but I know she still feels guilty for unknowingly being a part of it.

"Still haven't talked to him?" she asks.

It's my turn to frown. "No."

"Are you going to?"

"Eventually. I'm just still so…"

"Hurt?"

I nod. "Yeah."

"Can I ask you something?"

"Of course."

"Would you be this upset with him if you were still just friends?"

"Absolutely. The Cooper I've known for ten years never would have done what he did. Sure, he's always been bossy and a little pushy when it comes to breaking me out of my shell or whatever you want to call it, but he's never blatantly lied to me and gone behind my back. He's never made me feel betrayed before." I sigh. "I don't know. Maybe I'm just being dramatic about all of this. Maybe Cooper was right to do what he did."

"Um, no. You're not being dramatic," she insists. "I mean, it does probably hurt a little more now because you're in love with him, but that was *your* decision to sort through and you were clear about what you wanted. So, good intentions or not, he should have respected that, and he didn't. That's not okay. It's deceitful and you have every right to be pissed about it. I know I'd be big mad myself if Dean tried to pull some shit like that. I'd castrate him."

A grin pulls at my lips.

Poor Dean.

"I get where you're coming from. This place"—she waves her hand around the boutique—"is my passion. Designing is yours. You don't fuck with someone's passion."

"Thank you. I'm glad you understand."

"I do."

I tilt my head, eyeing her. "Why do I feel like you're about to say *but*?"

"I'm not. No *but*." She clears her throat. "*However*, I do think you need to talk to him and tell him where you're at with this. Talk it out. Because trust me, communication is key in a relationship. It makes all the difference."

Be open. Communicate more now than you ever have. It'll save a world of hurt because there are things at stake now that weren't before.

Momma B's words filter through my mind.

She's right, and so is River.

"Oh! Idea!" River says, clapping her hands together. "Since you're hating on the day-drinking in the office, how about we go out tonight? You, me, and Maya. Let's have some drinks, talk. Maybe dance. Maybe getting out of your apartment for something other than work will help. Clear your mind and all."

"I don't know…"

"Come on," she urges. "It'll be fun. We *never* go out."

This is true. Mostly because I'd rather be at home.

Except for maybe tonight.

I do need to talk to Cooper…

But perhaps a few drinks will help me clear my mind.

Tomorrow. I'll talk to him tomorrow.

"Okay. I'm in."

OF COURSE THIS is the place she'd pick to go drinking at.

I stare at the door of Lorde's, the bar where Cooper first kissed me, afraid to step inside because I know all I'm going to do all night is think about him when that's just what I'm trying *not* to do.

It's on the tip of my tongue to tell her there's no way in hell I'm going inside, but Maya looks like she needs a drink just as much as I do, and this night doesn't need to be all about my woes.

"Oh, thank god!" she cries. "We're here. I need a drink *pronto*."

"I think we all do," River agrees. "Also, I heard this place does karaoke on Fridays. Think we'll get drunk enough to try it?"

"Shit. I hope so," Maya says, pulling the door open.

We show our IDs to the guy at the entrance, then shuffle inside. It's loud as usual, and there are bodies everywhere it seems.

Guess we aren't the only ones running from our problems.

"I don't know what the hell I'm going to do," Maya complains when we reach the bar. She lifts her hand to signal the bartender. "I can't believe they're selling my apartment building to turn it into a damn outdoor sports equipment shop. Like we need *another* one of those."

"You and Sam can stay with us. I know Dean wouldn't have any issue with it."

Maya scoffs. "You really want me and my twelve-year-old to live in your two-bedroom apartment with you, your boyfriend, your demon cat, and his *emotional support turtle*?"

"First of all, Morris is *not* a demon. He only hates Dean. Second, it's only temporary, and you're my best friend. It's my job to help take care of you."

"And I love you for that, but we both know there's no way

that's going to work out." Maya sighs. "I'll figure something out. I *have* to figure something out."

"You will," I tell her, rubbing her back. "We'll help you look. We'll start tomorrow."

"Thank you." She blows out a breath. "I'm glad I have you two."

We both send her reassuring smiles.

"Hey, sorry about that," the bartender says, sliding up to the counter. "What can I—oh, Caroline, hey."

I turn at the sound of my name.

"Hey, Shayla," I say. "How are you?"

"Good, good. I was wondering if you were around here tonight."

I lift an eyebrow, curious.

She tips her head toward the other end of the bar. "Cooper didn't order your drink earlier."

Cooper's here?

Like she's summoned his attention, I can feel his eyes on me, burning right through me, straight to my heart.

I could smack myself. I've been in such a haze this week, I completely forgot today is Friday. And not just any Friday.

"It's Friday night out," I say.

She nods. "Yep. The gang's all here, as per usual. They're putting everything on Eli's tab again too. I guess this is the second time this month he's messed up hours' worth of work."

He did?

There's a twist in my gut. Shayla knows more about Cooper's job than I do currently.

I hate it.

"Anyway," she moves on, "want your usual?"

I nod. "Please. And whatever these two want."

She takes River's and Maya's drink orders, then hurries away.

Don't look. Don't look. Don't look.

I look.

Our eyes lock.

Everything falls away.

The bar, the loud music, the dancing bodies…it's all gone.

It's just us.

God do I miss that.

I miss his touch. His laugh. His kisses.

I miss *him*.

He lifts his drink to his lips, taking a sip but never pulling his eyes away from me, almost like he's challenging me to look away first.

I do.

I toss my hair over my shoulder and turn back to the bar, seeing Shayla's dropped off our drinks.

I pick mine up and instantly take a healthy swig.

"Caroline…" River says quietly when I turn back around. "We can go if you want. This is supposed to be a night about clearing your head, not being forced to deal with your issues."

"No." I shake my head. "It's fine. *I'm* fine."

"Good." She smiles. "Now, let's drink."

"Oh, wait! Let's do a toast," Maya says.

"To what?"

She lifts her glass, and River and I follow suit.

"To dumbasses—men *and* landlords!"

And we drink.

Chapter 19

COOPER

CAROLINE'S HERE.

I felt her the moment she walked in the door.

She didn't notice me, but I noticed her. My eyes tracked her as she moved through the crowd and to the bar, River and Maya at her side.

My hand clenches around the drink I'm holding. Paul's talking in my ear, but I don't hear him.

She's all I can see.

She must have stopped by the apartment before she came because this sure as hell isn't what she was wearing this morning.

A new navy blue dress I haven't seen before stops mid-thigh, hugging every inch of her body. There's a slit cut up the side that gives the most delectable glimpse of her skin, and she's wearing those fucking boots I *still* haven't gotten to take off her.

I want to wrap a jacket around her and strip her bare all at once.

I have to fight with myself to not stalk over to her and demand her attention.

I *need* her to talk to me. To hear me out.

Need her to know I love her and I don't want to go another minute without her.

I watch as she consoles Maya about something, then greets Shayla with a smile that lights up the fucking room even though I know she's hurting as badly as I am.

Then, she turns.

And our eyes lock.

I stop breathing.

I'm sorry, I say with my eyes. *I'm an idiot.*

I know, hers say back.

Then she flips the blonde locks I love to feel between my fingers over her shoulder and shuts me out again.

I let out a staggered breath, nearly choking on the air.

"You good?" Paul asks.

"Not even fucking close, man."

He follows my gaze. "Ah. Was wondering where she was tonight. You guys okay?"

I shrug. "I'm really not sure anymore."

"Damn. You fuck it up that fast?"

I glare at him and he laughs, not scared at all.

"Caroline's not the type of girl you let get away. She'll haunt your ass for the rest of your days. You'll turn into an old miserable fuck yelling at all the kids to get off your lawn."

Don't I fucking know it.

"All right!" The MC cuts through Paul's words. "Let's hear it for Henry, who never fails to woo us all with his rendition of Lady Gaga's 'Marry the Night.'"

The crowd cheers and whistles, clapping for Henry, a

regular here at Lorde's who always sings at least one Lady Gaga song.

"We're going to take a short karaoke break, but we'll be back soon with Joy, who promises to make us all swoon with their version of a popular love song."

The MC switches off the mic and sets it on the empty stool, the house music blaring back to life.

"Anyway," Paul continues, "whatever you did, you better apologize and make it grand."

Make her listen.

Dean's words echo in my mind.

I need to make her listen.

I need to make it grand.

I spring from my stool and push through the dancing crowd.

My feet don't stop until I'm standing on the stage, microphone in hand, looking out at the wild sea of people.

The MC rushes me.

"Hey, dude. I know you're probably excited to sing, but we're taking a break and we have a waiting list we follow. You'll need to wait your turn."

He reaches for the microphone and I pull it back.

"Please. I just need it for a few minutes."

"Sorry, no can do."

"*Please.* I… Just please."

He must see something in my eyes because he nods. "What do you need me to do?"

I whisper my plan into his ear, and he agrees.

"I'll kill the music," he says. "Good luck."

The MC flips the music off and the crowd groans, complaining loudly, throwing daggers my way.

I don't care about their attention.

I only want hers.

I flip the switch to *on* and the feedback screeches through the bar, drawing the eyes of just about every person in here.

"Shit. Fuck. Sorry."

A few scattered laughs.

I hold the microphone down by my leg, taking a few steadying breaths.

"Shit or get off the pot, asshole!" someone yells.

I flip him off.

More laughs.

The entire bar is watching me raptly, wondering what I'm doing up here.

Make her listen.

I take one more deep breath, then lift the mic to my mouth.

"I'm an idiot."

"We know!" another patron calls out.

I ignore them. "I've been lying to myself and everyone I know for a really long time."

"Holy shit. Is he coming out to us?" another voice asks.

"Lord, I hope so," a guy in the front answers, fanning himself.

"No dice. Sorry."

I wink at him and he frowns. I chuckle, continuing.

"The lying started when I was fifteen and the most beautiful girl I've ever laid eyes on moved in across the street. I was drawn to her instantly. One of those *had*-to-know-her kind of things, you know?" I tuck my hand into my pocket, trying to hide my shaking hands. "So that's what I did. I got to know her. Forced her to be my friend is more like it. Why she took pity on the annoying-as-hell neighbor kid is beyond me, but she did."

I grin, shaking my head at the memory.

"Anyway, so we became friends, right? And I thought, *This is enough. This is all I'll ever need to be happy. Her.*"

A few people in the crowd let out a collective *Aww.*

"The more I got to know her, the more I liked her. Whip-smart. Funny. And, most importantly, a good human. Kind. Shy. She was like sunshine, and I was drawn to her warmth. I wanted to keep it forever. I thought I was in love with her, and I thought she loved me too. I mean, that *had* to be why she kept me around, right? So, I did the next logical thing—kissed her...and it turned out she did *not* feel the same way *at all.* But it was fine. I played it off as an accident and she was none the wiser. No harm, no foul."

A few more scattered laughs.

"We stayed friends through high school. Moved away for college together. All the highs and lows of the life of a young twentysomething. Signing your first lease on a crappy apartment. Falling in love for the first time—for real. The inevitable *Holy shit I hate what I went to college for, now what the fuck am I going to do* moment we all have. Moving out of the crappy apartment and getting your first real nice place. All the really fun shit, you know?"

"Preach!" someone shouts.

"We were good. Golden. Best fucking friends forever. Nothing was ever going to touch us. Then she saw me naked and groped me, but that's a story for another day.

"Something shifted between us. Something became impossibly clear. I wanted her. So, I took a page out of fifteen-year-old me's book and I kissed her. Right here in this very bar." I point toward the hallway. "Back there. That's where my heart stopped beating, because this time? She kissed me back, and we didn't stop there."

"Yesssss!"

A whistle.

A few claps.

"What happened next?"

"I spent the last month and some change being happier than I have ever been." I run my hand through my hair, hanging my head. "Until I fucked it all up."

"I knew it!" someone hollers, and several people murmur their agreements, scoffing at me.

"I warned you I was an idiot," I answer. "I screwed up and now she's not talking to me. Shutting me out. And I get it—I deserve it. I meddled when I shouldn't have. Disrespected her. *Lied* to her. But like I said at the beginning of this, I've been doing that for the last ten years."

I lift my head, and I look over the crowd and right into Caroline's eyes for the first time.

She's staring back at me. Her blue eyes are wide, full of surprise and a little trepidation. Even from here, I can see the pink on her cheeks as everyone turns to stare at her, trying to get a peek at the girl I'm talking to.

"Accidents don't just happen accidentally. That kiss when we were fifteen? That wasn't an accident. I meant it. I meant it then, I mean it now. I've meant it for the last decade. Because, Caroline Elaine Reed"—her lips tic up when I say the wrong middle name—"I'm in love with you. *Hopelessly*."

Chapter 20

CAROLINE

I'VE BEEN SHAKING since the moment Cooper took the stage.

My cheeks are on fire, and at first, I had the urge to run and hide, but I couldn't look away from him.

I don't think I've taken a full breath the entire time he's been up there, recounting our friendship over the years. Talking about what's happened between us. Admitting his failures for all to hear.

Cooper is in love with me.

"Holy shit," River mutters. "I think he's going to sing."

I snap out of my stupor, just as the familiar licks of Olivia Newton-John's "Hopelessly Devoted to You" begin to play.

Oh god.

He lifts the microphone to his mouth and starts the first line.

And it's *awful.*

If Cooper thinks my singing sounds like three cats dying, his sounds like ten.

The crowd is a mixture of booing, laughing, cheering, and singing along.

Half of them are still staring at me, and for the first time ever, I don't care.

No matter how awful it is, I can't take my eyes off Cooper, and he can't take his eyes off me.

It's ridiculous.

Embarrassing.

And I love every single second of it.

He sings every word—horribly—and doesn't walk off the stage until the last chords fade away.

Everyone erupts into applause, clapping his back and high-fiving him as he pushes his way through the crowd.

"Well, that was some speech," the MC says into the mic. "Let's give a round of applause to our idiot of the evening!" Everyone cheers again. "Good luck, kid. Sounds like you're going to need it. Now, let's get back to the music, shall we?"

The house music fires back up as Cooper emerges from the throngs of people, striding toward me.

His usual confident swagger is missing, and he looks more vulnerable than I've ever seen him.

"Uh, we're going to give you two a moment," River says.

"Boo," Maya complains. "I totally want to hear what he's going to say."

River grabs her arm and they move down the bar, but I know they're still watching us closely.

"Hi," he says quietly, and it's the first thing he's directly said to me in days.

"Hi," I echo, and I swear I see relief in his eyes.

"Caroline…" He reaches for me but thinks better of it and drops his hand.

I hate that he drops his hand.

I *need* him to touch me. I need to feel him.

"Fuck," he mutters. "Everyone's watching us."

He looks around, scowling at the crowd who is still gathered close and obviously waiting to see what happens, but nobody cares. They just keep watching.

He steps into me, dipping his head low so only I can hear him.

His familiar scent of sage and summer hits me, and it's not just my hands shaking anymore.

It's my heart.

"I'm sorry," he says, his light green eyes finding mine. "I fucked up. I shouldn't have done what I did. I shouldn't have lied. Because I did—I lied right to you when I said I'd drop it. I had no intention of doing so, and that was wrong. I *should* have dropped it. I…I just…"

He runs his tongue over his lips, and I swear he mouths the word *fuck*.

"It was hard, you know," he continues. "Seeing you throwing away your shot at your dreams killed me. I've watched you do it too many times over the years, and I couldn't do it again. But that doesn't make what I did okay because it wasn't about me. It was never about me. It was about you. I know that, and I'm sorry I took your day away from you. I'm sorry I pushed you. I'm sorry I lied. I'm sorry. I didn't treat you as a friend, and I certainly didn't treat you as a partner."

He takes another step closer, and I hold my breath.

"If you're willing to give me another chance, I promise I will never, *ever* disrespect you again."

I hate hearing him admit he lied and knew what he was

doing. Hate hearing that it was a calculated decision. It hurts all over again.

But...I believe him.

He's sorry, and I believe that.

Tired of the audience, I grab his hand, pulling him toward the hallway where he first kissed me.

I drop his hand when we're alone, turning around to face him.

"I'm still mad at you, Cooper," I tell him. "I want you to understand that. I'm still hurt, and this is something that's going to hurt for a while. It felt like my dreams and my desires didn't matter to you unless I was doing them the way *you* wanted them done, and I need to know they matter, especially to you."

"Your dreams matter to me, Caroline, and I'm sorry I ever made you feel differently. You're the most important person in my life. Not just as a girlfriend, but as a friend. And I don't want to lose you as either."

His eyes are pained, yet full of hope.

And I break.

I dive into his arms, and he catches me eagerly, wrapping his warmth around me like my favorite blanket.

His lips find mine and suddenly I'm pressed against the wall. He's kissing me hard and fast, like he's scared he'll never get to do it again.

He kisses me for all the days he didn't. For all the ways he hurt me and for all the ways he loves me.

His fevered touches turn languid until we're barely kissing at all, just holding our lips together.

"Did you mean what you said up there?" I ask. "About being in love with me?"

"Hopelessly."

I smile against him. "Your singing is god-awful."

"That was so fucking embarrassing."

"But you did it anyway. For me."

"For you." He presses his forehead against mine. "Because I've never felt this way about anyone before. I've never wanted this with anyone more than I want this with you. I love you, Caroline Josephine Reed."

"That's not my middle name."

"No, but it should be. I think it's my favorite one yet."

I roll my eyes, and he tightens his hold on my hips. "Don't roll your eyes at me."

I do it again.

"Caroline…"

"Cooper…" I mock.

He shakes his head, smiling.

God, I've missed his smile.

He pulls back, eyes meeting mine. "Can you forgive me for being a colossal idiot?"

"Jury's still out."

"What can I do to help my case?"

"Hmm…" I tap my chin. "I'm not sure."

"Well, I've got a few ideas…"

He captures my mouth again, pressing against me in all the delicious spots I've missed him.

I have no idea how long we stay like that, locked together in a kiss. People come and go around us, but we're lost in our own world.

When we finally come up for air, we're both smiling.

"I love you," he says, brushing a stray hair from my face.

243

"And I'm sorry if that's too much or too scary, but it's true. If you need time, I understand. I—"

"I love you too," I blurt.

His face lights up. "Yeah?"

I nod, then whisper...

"*Hopelessly.*"

Epilogue

COOPER

Five months later

"COME ON, Coop! It's pizza and movie night."

"I know, I know."

She huffs. "A good *boyfriend* would be in here with his girlfriend already."

That little...

"The whole reason I'm still in here working well after business hours is because *someone* kept me distracted this morning and I was late. A good *girlfriend* would have let him work. This is *your* fault."

"I'm sorry, are you really sitting there complaining about a morning blow job?"

"Yes. When it interferes with my livelihood, yes. Someone has to pay for all these bills you run up, you know."

She grumbles something I can't quite make out, but I know she definitely calls me an asshole.

I chuckle. "Give me five more minutes!"

"That's what you said five minutes ago."

"Sucks when you're the one waiting, doesn't it?"

She growls, and I hear her shuffling around, probably grabbing her chinchilla blanket and curling up in a ball on the couch.

I hear *The Vampire Diaries* start ten seconds later.

I'm sure she's sitting there with her sketchpad on her lap, hand flying over the page as she cooks up whatever ideas are brewing in her mind.

After the success of the festival, Caroline *finally* agreed to put her designs on the shop's website.

The launch was huge and, much to her surprise but nobody else's, she sold out in less than a day.

She now has her own section of the store *and* a dedicated line on the website.

Basically, she's fucking killing it and proving her dad wrong.

I couldn't be prouder of her.

I hit save on the code I was looking over. The game we've been working on for nearly a year now is set to come out in two months, and we've been cleaning up all the bugs the test players have found. It's led to long nights and even longer weekends, but I'm excited about how it's going to do, especially since the reception has been fantastic so far.

"It's been five minutes…" she calls.

With a grin, I push away from my desk and pad down the hall.

"I'm done," I say, coming into the living room. "Are you happy?"

She tosses her sketchpad aside and looks up at me with excited eyes. "Yes. Now can we order pizza? I'm *starving*."

"Hi, starving. I'm Cooper."

She grins, then rolls her eyes at me.

"Don't roll your eyes at me. You know what that does to me, and if you're so hungry, I highly doubt you want me to get distracted right now."

"Fair point." She gets up off the couch, her favorite gray blanket falling from her shoulders. "Can we order breadsticks too?"

"I suppose," I say as she grabs her phone, ready to place our order. "I mean, it *is* a special day and all."

"It is?" She wrinkles her nose, stopping what she's doing. "Why?"

I lift a brow. "You don't remember?"

"Um...no?" She looks at me pointedly. "I swear if this is your way of telling me it's my turn to take the trash out again, I'm going to order breadsticks *and* dessert."

"It's not the trash."

"Then what is it?"

"Wow. You really don't know, do you?" She sighs, and I smirk. "I'm hurt you wouldn't remember this day."

"Cooper..." she warns, crossing her arms over her chest. "You're starting to test my patience."

"What are you going to do about it? Tap your foot at me like you are now?"

"No. I'll...I'll...withhold sex."

"Oh, taking a page out of my book now, huh?"

"Yes."

I laugh, crossing the room to her, wrapping my arms around her waist.

"Come on, Care. Think. What happened about...say...six months ago?"

Her brows scrunch together as she thinks back. "Umm... we started dating?"

"Keep going."

"Your favorite sports team won some fancy trophy?"

"Try again…"

She growls. "Ugh. I don't know. Nothing is sticking out to me. I—"

It hits her.

"*Oh my god*, Cooper. Did you really?"

I nod.

"Is that why you got me flowers this morning? Brought me breakfast in bed?"

"Yes."

"You put the day I *accidentally* touched your penis into your calendar so you could remind me of it six months later?"

"Oh, Care. We both know accidents don't just happen accidentally."

"I cannot believe you."

"Yes, you can."

"You… You're *exhausting*."

"I know." I laugh, pressing a quick kiss to her lips. "But you love me."

"I do."

"And I love you too. *Hopelessly*."

"Ugh…" She shakes her head, trying hard to fight the smile that wants to break free.

And then, she rolls her eyes.

We never do order pizza.

Other Titles by Teagan Hunter

CAROLINA COMETS

Puck Shy

ROOMMATE ROMPS SERIES

Loathe Thy Neighbor

Love Thy Neighbor

Crave Thy Neighbor

Tempt Thy Neighbor

SLICE SERIES

A Pizza My Heart

I Knead You Tonight

Doughn't Let Me Go

A Slice of Love

Cheesy on the Eyes

TEXTING SERIES

Let's Get Textual

I Wanna Text You Up

Can't Text This

Text Me Baby One More Time

INTERCONNECTED STANDALONES

We Are the Stars

If You Say So

HERE'S TO SERIES

Here's to Tomorrow

Here's to Yesterday

Here's to Forever: A Novella

Here's to Now

Want to be part of a fun reader group, gain access to exclusive content and giveaways, and get to know me more?

Join Teagan's Tidbits on Facebook!

Want to stay on top of my new releases?

Sign up for New Release Alerts!

Acknowledgments

This time, the acknowledgments section is solely for you, Reader.

I'm writing this in November 2020 and if you know... well, you know.

Though it consists of twelve months just like any other year, it seems far longer than that.

It's been lonely and exhausting. Too many people have lost loved ones. Too many people have lost themselves. It's a lot to take in. A lot to push through.

But we're doing it. We're all doing it. We're moving forward, making the best of it. Thank you for giving me just a few hours of your attention. I truly hope that during these crazy unprecedented times, you've been able to find some love and laughter. And that maybe you even found some laughter between these pages.

I usually end all of my acknowledgments pages with the same thing: *With love and unwavering gratitude.*

Just know this year I mean it even more.

Thank you.
Teagan

About the Author

TEAGAN HUNTER is a Missouri-raised gal, but currently lives in South Carolina with her Marine veteran husband, where she spends her days begging him for a cat. She survives off of coffee, pizza, and sarcasm. When not writing, you can find her binge-watching *Supernatural* or *One Tree Hill*. She enjoys cold weather, buys more paperbacks than she'll ever read, and never says no to brownies.

www.teaganhunterwrites.com